HAUNTED HEARTS

SUZANA THOMPSON

ISBN 9781959834199

CHAPTER 1

almost didn't go to school that day. My sleep had been filled with restless dreams I couldn't remember—except for being scared and running away from someone or something. I convinced myself that the bad feeling I had was just a remnant from those nightmares and didn't mean anything.

Also, it was Friday, and I was going on a date. I couldn't call off sick from school and then expect my parents to let me go out that evening. So, I put on a pretty, light pink top and a pair of jean shorts. We were only two weeks into school, and the weather made it feel like it was still summer.

The sun had given me tan skin and my first boyfriend. Matt had been a lifeguard at the pool where I'd spent the majority of my summer vacation, and he'd asked me out in July. Since he was popular, I hadn't expected him to still be with me once school started. That was why I hadn't gotten attached to him, why I hadn't gone all in on our relationship.

Liar, a voice in my mind whispered. *You know why your heart's not in it.*

I ignored my subconscious as I walked out of my house and got into Matt's car. He'd been driving me to school and driving me home, which was so much better than taking the bus. That wasn't why I liked him though. Matt was genuinely a nice guy, despite his looks, popularity, and athletic ability. He'd been on our school's baseball team since Freshman year, and he was apparently really good. So much so that he was likely to get a college scholarship for it before we graduated. I'd never been to one of his games, but I was planning to go this year once baseball season started in the spring. That was still many months away, since it was only the beginning of September.

Matt smiled at me, and it was a bright, sunny smile. He had blond hair and blue eyes, and I guessed that I'd always associate him with summer. Not only because our relationship had started during the summer, but because of his happy disposition. He had a golden glow and exuded warmth and happiness.

It should have outshone the dark, brooding magnetism of my secret crush, but it didn't. Why was I so drawn to a guy who was so unapproachable? Yet he radiated this intense, powerful energy that caught my attention anytime he was near.

My eyes had been riveted to him the first time I saw him on my first day of high school. The rest of the people in the hallway had faded into the background as I stood staring at him. His hair was black as midnight, and his eyes were almost as dark. I was struck by a feeling of recognition, although I knew that I had never seen him before. I would have remembered his striking dark beauty and powerful presence. I felt it even then, when we were fresh-faced, excited teens on our first day of high school. Well, I was excited. He was aloof and coolly confident, like a person who was much older than the rest of us, although he didn't look it. I later found out that he was the same age as me, and strangely enough was also born on the exact same day.

While I stood watching him with arrested attention during our first encounter, his dark eyes had skimmed over me as he moved toward me in his motorized wheelchair. His gaze had traveled back up to my face and held mine, and I hadn't been able to look away. Time seemed to stop while my heart raced at an alarming speed. I'd stared at him as he closed the distance between us.

His neutral expression never changed as he came to a stop in front of me. After holding my gaze for a moment, he finally said, "You're blocking my locker."

I noted how deep and masculine his voice was, and then I realized that he was waiting for me to move. "Sorry," I said as I stepped aside.

He hadn't acknowledged my apology or spared me another glance, and the sting of rejection had quickened my steps away from him.

That had been three years ago, and my crush on him hadn't abated despite that being our only interaction. A sane person would have given up hope by then, but what kept me hooked was that he didn't completely ignore me. Sometimes I would catch him looking at me with a thrilling intensity that made me think that he was interested in me. Yet he had never smiled back at me when I had smiled at him to let him know I liked him. He'd only stared at me for another moment before looking away.

I'd thought that maybe he was shy, although there was nothing timid about him. Still, wishful thinking had convinced me that I needed to try approaching him. After all, it had been a couple of years since our first encounter. So, I'd worked up the courage and started toward him the next time he directed that intense stare at me. It had been just as I'd exited the lunch line with my tray of food, and he'd caught my eye across the cafeteria. I'd halted and taken a fortifying breath before striding toward him like I was on a mission.

He'd watched me, his gaze like a dare. He'd waited until I'd walked past my usual table, until I'd crossed the cafeteria, until it was clear to anyone that I was headed directly to where he sat alone by choice. When I was only steps away from his table, his expression shifted to cold and unapproachable. I'd halted, losing my nerve as he regarded me with all the warmth of a polar ice cap. He'd then looked down at whatever book he was reading and hadn't glanced back up. Humiliation had swept over me, and I'd felt like a fool standing there while he ignored me.

Since his table was at the edge of the cafeteria, I couldn't walk past it and pretend that I was on my way to one beyond his. If I hadn't been holding my lunch tray, I could have just continued on to the exit and escaped into the hallway. Instead, I was forced to turn around and head back past all the people who had seen me try to sit with him and get rejected. They had definitely noticed, because I felt their eyes on me.

Even worse, my friends had seen it too, since they'd spotted me walking past our table and had then watched to see where I was going. My best friend, Abby, informed me of this as soon as I set down my tray.

"Wow, Hazel, you've got guts! When I saw you going by, I was wondering what the heck you were doing. But when I saw where you were going, I couldn't believe it. I didn't know you liked Devon. Why didn't you tell me?"

"I don't," I lied. "I was just trying to be friendly. He sits by himself every day, and I thought maybe he could use a friend."

"You don't have to be embarrassed about liking him," our friend, Sarah, assured me. "Lots of girls do."

"Yeah," Emily agreed.

Apparently, nobody was buying my denial. I had to admit that my excuse for approaching him had been weak. Devon Culver was only lacking friends because he'd withdrawn from them. He'd been popular sophomore year when he'd emerged from his self-imposed exile from socializing. He was invited to parties, sat at the popular table in the cafeteria, and had hooked up with several girls.

I didn't like to think about that. Partly because it made me feel like an ass for assuming that he couldn't have sex, and partly because I was jealous. Not that I wanted to hook up with him. That was something I hadn't done with anyone yet, and I wanted to be in a relationship when it happened. None of those girls were in a relationship with Devon.

I had no idea why he didn't have a girlfriend, and why he'd stopped socializing with the popular people. I had heard that he used to go to private school before his accident. He'd been only thirteen years old when he'd ended up in a wheelchair after surviving the car crash that killed his twin brother and his mom.

I wondered what he was like before that. Had he been more approachable? Somehow, I couldn't imagine him ever being warm and friendly. Maybe his aloofness was bred into him, since he was born into one of the oldest and most distinguished families in Salem.

We lived in Salem. Yep, that Salem. I wished that I was a witch, but I wasn't. Of course not, because that would have made me interesting, and I was completely unremarkable. The total opposite of Devon, who could definitely be mistaken for a warlock. Except for my name—Hazel Guthrie. That sounded witchy. Too bad I didn't match my name. I didn't even have hazel eyes. They were brown. A warm, friendly brown. Not intimidating at all.

Not like Devon's eyes. They were brown too, but it was such a dark brown that they looked almost black. They were beautiful, of course, just like the rest of him, but intimidating—just like the rest of him. Maybe it was the cold look in them. His eyes never looked warm and friendly.

So why did I feel so drawn to him? Why did I look forward to seeing him every day at school and being in his presence? Why was it more exciting than being with my boyfriend?

I was a terrible girlfriend who didn't deserve him. I shouldn't be infatuated with another guy while I was dating him, but my crush on Devon predated my relationship with Matt. That was how I justified it to myself. It wasn't like I developed the crush after Matt asked me out. It already existed—and it was unrequited. So, it was harmless. It wasn't like Devon was suddenly going to be interested in me when he hadn't been for the past three years. It wasn't like this year was going to be any different.

He apparently wasn't interested in anyone anymore. After that interlude of socializing during sophomore year, he'd suddenly shut everyone out again and returned to being a loner. Now I was actually more popular than him, but only because I was dating Matt. He was the complete opposite of Devon— blond, blue-eyed, athletic, and easygoing. Everyone liked him, and I knew that I was lucky that he had chosen me. I was hoping to finally begin dating that year after deciding that I wasn't going to waste any more time pining after Devon. This time, my wish was fulfilled. Matt had been working as a lifeguard at the pool, and he'd asked me out about a month after summer break began.

Suddenly, I was going on dates, experiencing my first kiss, and even going to Homecoming. I had been having the senior year of my dreams. So why did I still feel like something was missing?

Why was I still so aware of Devon?

"Earth to Hazel."

"Hmm?" I looked at my best friend, Abby.

"Sorry to interrupt your fantasies," she said.

I startled. "What?" Had I spoken his name aloud?

"Speak of the devil, here he comes."

With the excitement I always had when I saw Devon, I turned in my seat to see Matt approaching our table. Feeling guilty, I smiled at him.

"Hey, Hazel." He leaned down to give me a quick peck on the lips.

I was surprised to see him, because we didn't have the same lunch. "How are you here?"

"We got out of class a little early for good behavior. Substitute today. Just wanted to stop and see you."

The bell rang just then, and I automatically stood up in response.

He gave me a wry smile. "I guess that's all the time we have. Too bad we don't have lunch together."

"Yeah," I agreed, although I was secretly glad that we didn't. I was comfortable sitting with my friends, and I liked to steal glances at Devon.

The guilt hit me again, and I picked up my tray. "Okay, see you later."

"I'll get that for you," he said as he took my tray.

"Thanks," I told him and took a step back in preparation of taking my leave. He was staying there, because he had lunch now.

He smiled warmly at me. "See you after school."

I returned his smile and turned to go. Abby walked out of the cafeteria with me and gushed, "He's such a great boyfriend."

"He is," I agreed. *And I'm a terrible girlfriend.*

"Maybe you'll get married one day," she continued.

That kind of talk made me uncomfortable. "We've only been dating for three months. Let's not plan a wedding just yet."

"At least not before prom," she joked.

We had to part ways then, because our classes were on opposite sides of the building. I turned to walk down the hall and bumped into Devon, losing my balance and almost falling into his lap. His hands shot out to steady me.

"Sorry," I said, mortified at my clumsiness.

He stared at me without saying anything, increasing my embarrassment. My face flamed as I hastily righted myself, and he let go of my arms while keeping his unnerving stare on me. After a prolonged beat, he glided around me and continued on his way like nothing had happened.

That wasn't as easy for me to do, partly because I was embarrassed, but also because he touched me. I remembered the feel of his hands on my arms, and my stomach fluttered. He also smelled really good. It must have been some expensive cologne that he wore. He definitely didn't drench himself in it, because the tantalizing scent was only noticeable due to my nearness to him. It was like it was drawing me closer, tempting me to sniff him more fully. Luckily, I had resisted and saved myself from further embarrassment.

What happened in my last class of the day made the hallway incident pale by comparison. Devon was in two of my classes, which I had considered a gift from the gods. I got to see him in my first class and my last, so I started and ended my day with him. On that day he stopped and dropped a folded piece of paper on my desk before heading to his own without saying a word.

My heart pounded as I stared at it, hardly daring to believe it was a note from him. Finally, I picked it up and opened it with unsteady hands.

Hazel,

I will drive you home today.

I read those few words over and over again, not believing what I was seeing. When the teacher began speaking, I quickly slipped the note between the pages of my textbook. Stealthily, I texted Matt while the teacher wasn't looking. He had been my usual ride home since we started dating. All I told him in my message was that I couldn't ride home with him and would explain later. I had no idea what I was going to say to him, but I wasn't turning down an invitation from Devon.

It turned out to be the most awkward experience of my life. He didn't say a word to me after asking me for my address. I had been planning to give him directions, but he typed it into his GPS. The automated voice telling him where to turn was the only sound in the vehicle. I was not usually a shy person, but Devon had an unapproachable vibe. What could I say to him? *Why did you decide to give me a ride home today after pretty much ignoring me all these years?* I had the silly urge to give him a note like kids did in elementary school. Do you like me? Check yes or no.

His neutral expression certainly gave me no clue as he kept his eyes on the road. I was still trying to work up the courage to start a conversation with him when we arrived at my house. Throwing caution to the wind, I asked, "Would you like to come in?" If that didn't make it obvious that I liked him, nothing would.

He looked at me then, and my pulse jumped as he reached out to touch my arm. His hand remained there as he closed his eyes for a moment. When he opened them, he pulled his hand back and said, "No, thank you."

My face heated, because his rejection of me was obvious. "Well, thanks for the ride," I managed before hastily getting out of his truck. I wasn't so graceful, because I had to hop down off the foot rail.

No sooner did I close the passenger door and step back, and he was pulling out of my driveway. I stood there watching him take off down the street and drive off out of sight. Why, I wondered. Why did he offer to drive me home today?

It was as much of an enigma to me as he was.

CHAPTER 2

I didn't get the terrible news until late that night. Matt never answered my text messages, so I assumed he was mad at me. Maybe he had found out that I ditched him to ride home with Devon. It wasn't surprising, since I had felt many eyes on us when I walked beside him through the school parking lot. I hadn't actually dared to look directly at them, but I knew that we were noticed.

When Matt didn't show up for our movie date later that evening, I knew for sure that he must be mad. He might even decide to break up with me, I thought. It was the first Friday evening that I didn't spend with him since we began dating.

I was still awake after eleven when my phone rang. Expecting it to be Matt, I was surprised to see that Abby was calling me. "Hello?"

"Hazel, oh my God!" she sobbed.

I thought immediately of her dad, who was a police officer. "What's wrong? Why are you crying?"

"I'm coming over." She hung up before I could say anything else.

My parents looked up from the TV as I entered the living room. "Abby is coming over. She sounds really upset."

"Oh no!" Mom responded, probably thinking the same thing I was.

That fear intensified when only Abby and her mom showed up at our house. "Hazel! You're really okay." Abby threw her arms around me in a fierce hug. "When Dad told me about Matt..."

I pulled back to look at her. "Your dad's okay?" Then what she said hit me. "Wait, what about Matt?"

Abby looked away from me, and her mom came to put an arm around my shoulders and gently guide me toward the loveseat. "Why don't you sit down?"

Something cold constricted my heart. "What happened to Matt?"

Abby started crying again. "There was an accident."

"Oh my God!" I pulled away from them and rushed to the entryway closet where I kept the shoes I wore the majority of the time.

My dad was the one who approached me as I tied my sneakers. "Honey, come sit down for a minute."

"I have to see him, Dad." I stood up from my crouch and saw his face. "Dad," I whispered.

"I'm sorry, Hazel," he said gently. "He didn't make it." He tried to put his arm around me, but I ran into the living room.

What he said was impossible. He had to be mistaken, because I just saw Matt earlier in the day. He came to say hi to me at lunch. He couldn't just suddenly be dead. I halted when I saw the expression on my mom's face. Abby's mom was trying to console her as she wept beside her on the loveseat. I ran to her and sank to my knees in front of her. "Tell them it's not true."

When Abby looked at me with her tear-stained face, I couldn't deny it any longer. I stared at her as I trembled with the horrible knowledge, and then my own tears came. Abby and her mom ended up staying that entire sleepless night. The funeral was on Tuesday, and most of the senior class attended. Besides going to that sad event, I stayed home the whole week.

I learned the details of the accident. A drunk driver slammed into Matt's car head-on as he drove home from school. The guy was going fifty in a twenty-five-mile zone when he drifted over into Matt's lane. He was killed instantly, but the drunk driver survived the crash and was taken to the hospital. His license had already been revoked for driving under the influence, but that hadn't stopped him from getting behind the wheel.

"Dad said that you would have been killed too if you had been in the car with Matt," Abby told me. She came over after the funeral, and we were talking in my room. She shuddered and took in a deep breath.

"Good thing Devon decided to give me a ride home," I retorted bitterly.

Her eyes widened. "What?"

That's when I confessed the whole thing to her. My guilt had been tearing me up, but telling her about my secret crush on Devon didn't make me feel any better. "I cheated on Matt."

Her blue eyes were huge. "You mean you and Devon..."

I sighed. "No, he just drove me home." Expelling a breath, I took another one in before saying, "I went off with Devon and left Matt to die."

"Didn't you hear me?" Abby demanded. "You would have been killed too! It's a miracle that Devon decided to give you a ride home. So, you had a crush on him. Who hasn't?"

She made it sound like my crush on him was in the past, when it was still ongoing while I was dating Matt. Guilt sliced through me like a knife. "I feel so awful. If only..."

I began to cry again. Abby hugged me, and I took comfort in her embrace. She was blinded by all our years of friendship and didn't see me as the horrible person I now knew I was.

She pulled back to look at me. "You're not the only one who feels guilty. When Dad told me you weren't in the car with Matt, I felt so relieved. I'm sad about Matt, but losing you would have been the worst."

I was so crushed by my guilt and grief over Matt that I hadn't thought about what would have happened if I hadn't accepted that ride from Devon. But I started to question all the events of that day. By the time I returned to school the following week, I was consumed with Devon's role in the tragedy.

I watched him at lunch and in the classes I had with him, but this time it was for a different reason than before. If he noticed my scrutiny, he didn't show it. My slow-building anger helped me get through the day, because I was swamped by well-meaning people who didn't know how guilty I felt every time they offered me their condolences. My teachers told me to take as much time as I needed with the make-up work from the week I had missed.

I was now past the point of tears and ready to confront Devon. When he arrived at his locker, I was waiting for him. "You knew," I accused him without preamble.

His dark eyes flitted toward me, but his expression betrayed nothing. That was all the attention he spared me before opening his locker door and calmly filling his backpack with the books he needed. I stood there fuming as he completed his task and closed the door. He left without saying a word.

It infuriated me, and I charged after him. "Why didn't you warn Matt?" I demanded as I came up beside him.

He moved out of the path of other students exiting the school and stopped next to the wall. "Your grief has made you irrational."

I was on the verge of hysteria as I let loose on him. "I'll tell you what's irrational. Liking someone who can't be bothered to care about anyone. God, I always thought you were so cool, but now I know you're as cold as ice."

For a moment, there seemed to be some kind of emotion in his eyes as he listened to my outburst, but then his neutral expression made me think I had imagined it. "I'm sorry for your loss," he said with all the feeling of a robot.

It was a clear conclusion to the conversation as he resumed his journey out of the school and into the parking lot. I was too fired up to be deterred, though, and I followed him to his truck. "No, scratch that. Ice has the ability to melt, but you're made of stone."

"I'll give you a ride home," was his only response.

"Why?" I taunted. "Is the bus going to crash too?"

The stare he fixed on me, combined with the tone of his voice, had a chilling effect. "I've made allowances for you in your distress, but I'm telling you to stop the hysterics right now."

This side of him went way beyond intimidating, and it completely unnerved me. He unlocked the doors. "Get in," he commanded in the same hard tone.

Suddenly wondering if I should run, I nevertheless sat down in the passenger seat and pulled the door shut. Buckling my seatbelt, I dared a glance at Devon, who was already settling in to drive. I stayed silent until he pulled out of the parking lot, and then I tried taking a different approach.

"I'm sorry I attacked you like that. You saved my life." When he didn't respond, I continued in a tentative tone. "I'm just wondering why you didn't warn Matt about what was going to happen."

He was silent for so long that I thought he wasn't going to answer. "How could I possibly know what was going to happen?"

"I don't know, but you did. Why else would you offer to drive me home on that exact day?"

"Maybe I like you," he said.

How many times had I fantasized about hearing him say those words to me? In the past I would have had hope that he actually meant it. "You don't act like you like me. You didn't even talk to me after you asked for my address."

"I lost my nerve." His eyes were still on the road as he drove.

All the fight had gone out of me. "Listen, I understand if you want to keep this a secret, but there's no one else here besides us. Why don't you just admit that you knew the accident was going to happen?"

"Because I didn't," he insisted.

With a heavy sigh, I turned away from him to stare out the window until we arrived at my house. "Thanks for the ride," I said, not bothering to glance at him.

"Hazel," he said, and I turned to see him looking at me. "Forget about these delusions."

He held my gaze for a moment and then looked away to signal that our conversation was finished.

I got out of his truck and started walking up the driveway without waiting for him to leave. He had failed to convince me that my conclusion was wrong, but it was clear that he wasn't going to admit the truth.

CHAPTER 3

More than a month passed before Devon spoke to me again. During that time, I often noticed him watching me at school. Maybe he was worried that I'd tell someone my suspicions about his psychic ability, but I hadn't even told Abby. If only he understood that he could trust me.

When Abby asked me about him giving me a ride home again, I said that he just felt sorry for me. However, she had been convinced that it meant he liked me. Other people thought that too, and rumors about us had circulated until they died down after he didn't interact with me again.

In the meantime, I had begun researching psychic phenomena. The possibility was fascinating, and there were even examples from history. I learned that Abraham Lincoln had a dream ten days before he was assassinated in which someone told him that the president was dead. That was creepy!

I wondered if Devon also had a premonition in a dream. That still didn't explain why he hadn't warned Matt about the crash. Then again, dreams were often vague, so maybe he didn't know that Matt was in danger too. My chances of finding out the truth were nonexistent, since he had denied the whole thing. I couldn't understand why, since it was an amazing ability. He had literally saved my life. Then I thought about Matt, and I found the reason for Devon's denial. Did he feel bad that he wasn't able to save him too? I knew that I would if I were in his shoes.

I was overwhelmed by sympathy for him. Why hadn't I realized this before?

The urge to comfort him was strong, and I waited impatiently until the end of the school day and followed him out of our last class. "It's not your fault," I blurted.

He maneuvered out of the flow of foot traffic and turned to face me. "What's your problem now?" he demanded.

"There's no problem," I assured him. "I just wanted you to know that it's not your fault that Matt died." I winced a little at mentioning his death, because it still hurt to acknowledge that he was dead. I would have rather avoided thinking about it.

"Of course it's not my fault," Devon said like I was stupid. "He was killed by a drunk driver."

I gritted my teeth, because I hated any mention of that guy. It was so unfair that he survived, while Matt—who was blameless in the accident, died. Struggling to get past my bitterness, I said, "I meant for not warning him. It's not your fault you didn't know he was in danger too."

There was a charged pause, and then he said, "Your friend is planning a surprise birthday party for you this evening."

I blinked at him, trying to comprehend what he was saying. The change of topic was confusing me.

"It's your birthday," he stated.

"Yes," I confirmed, still not getting where he was going with this. Then I wondered if this was another display of his psychic ability. "How did you know?"

"Abby invited me to your surprise party," he informed me.

I gaped at him. "She...what?"

He nodded. "It's tonight at her house. She invited me last week."

This was so not what I wanted, and he nodded as if in affirmation of it. "I told her you wouldn't want a party."

I had told her the same thing myself when she asked about my birthday party. She'd been upset that I didn't want to celebrate my eighteenth birthday, so I shouldn't have been so blindsided by this news. I thought I was compromising with her when I gave in to her demands to have a sleepover at her house. Instead, she had gone behind my back and planned a party.

"You don't have to go," Devon said, pulling me out of my thoughts.

I expelled a breath. "Yeah, I do. How's it going to look if I don't show up to my own party?"

"Why do you care?" he retorted. "It's not your problem that she decided to have this party without asking you."

I sighed. "She's just trying to cheer me up."

He snorted. "That'll work. You'll forget about your dead boyfriend."

I blinked at him, stunned by his callous remark.

"Am I wrong?" he challenged.

"No," I said slowly. "But that was..."

"Harsh? The truth usually is."

That statement gave me a glimpse into his perspective that I'd never had before. Something about his blunt attitude actually put me at ease with him. There was no awkwardness like there was with other people now, who all seemed not to know what to say to me anymore since Matt died. Maybe that was why I had no trouble asking Devon, "So, are you coming to my party?"

He eyed me for a long moment, and I met his speculative gaze head-on. Finally, he shrugged. "Sure."

Something leapt to life within me, but I kept my expression neutral. I sensed that I shouldn't linger after that, lest he change his mind. "Okay. See you." I took off for the exit and rode the bus home.

I then took a shower and rummaged through my closet for the perfect outfit to wear. I settled for a pleated black skirt and a fitted white sweater. When Abby saw me, she immediately knew that something was up.

"Who told you?" she demanded.

I tried to act clueless. "Told me what?"

"It was supposed to be a surprise," she whined.

"What was?"

She huffed in annoyance. "C'mon, Hazel, it's obvious you know. Why else would you dress up for a sleepover?"

I dropped the pretense. "Okay, I know you're having a party for me—even though I told you I didn't want one."

Her expression softened. "You should celebrate your birthday."

I looked away from her. "It doesn't feel right."

I heard her sigh. "It's okay to have fun on your birthday. On any day. You can't be sad all the time."

Her words were a dagger of guilt to my heart, because I didn't feel sad all the time. Not even a majority of the time. After the initial shock and heartbreak, during which I cried for days, I had gotten over my grief much faster than expected. Too fast. It had only been a little over a month, and Matt was already fading from my mind. So much so that I was trying to look pretty for another guy.

"It's okay to move on," Abby said, and I glanced at her in surprise.

She gave me an affectionate smile. "You never dress up unless it's to impress a guy, or if your mom forces you. I'm guessing she didn't force you to look nice for a sleepover at my house."

Guilt sliced through me again. "It's Devon," I admitted.

Her mouth dropped open in surprise. "He told you about the party?"

"Yeah, he said you invited him." I gave her a reproachful look. "I can't believe you did that behind my back."

"I wanted to cheer you up," she said defensively. "But, uh..."

She trailed off and glanced warily at my outfit. "He said he can't come to the party," she said with a wince.

I snorted. "There's no way he was that polite about it. He probably just flat out told you no. I mean literally just the one word. Am I right?"

She gaped at me, and I knew that I had guessed correctly.

Abby's expression morphed into outrage. "So, he told you about the party just to ruin the surprise. What a..."

She huffed and then said haughtily, "Well, being a Christian woman, I can't say it."

This elicited a genuine laugh out of me. We both started quoting this line from the Wizard of Oz after we watched it for the first time since we were kids about a year ago. We hadn't noticed it when we were younger, but we got a kick out of it when we were old enough to appreciate it and understand its reference to swearing. "I'd love to hear you tell him that. He probably wouldn't know what to say."

She lifted her nose in the air. "I'm not speaking to him at all."

"So, you're going to ignore your guest?" I questioned casually.

Her gaze snapped to mine. "What?"

"He told me he's coming to the party," I informed her.

Her eyes widened. "For real?"

"Yep," I replied.

A panicked kind of excitement overtook her. "We have to go! How could you not tell me this right away? Oh my God, I left Emily and Sarah in charge of the party. They're going to freak when they see him!"

"As opposed to how calm you're being," I remarked drily.

"We have to go!" she exclaimed again and yanked the door open to run outside to her car.

I smiled and shook my head before grabbing my duffle bag that contained all my overnight necessities. I made sure that the door locked behind me, because my parents had decided to go out when they found out I was spending the evening at Abby's house. They were taking me out for my birthday the following day instead.

The drive to Abby's house was fraught with the tension emanating from her. She managed to make me nervous too after she reminded me several times to act surprised.

Just as we got out of her car, I recognized Devon's truck pulling into the driveway behind us. He exited it quickly, with his nifty wheelchair lift depositing him on the pavement straight from the driver's seat.

Abby apparently forgot herself as she placed her hands on her hips and admonished him, "You're late. You'd ruin the surprise for Hazel if you hadn't already done that."

He shrugged nonchalantly. "I told you she didn't want a party."

"Oh, you know her better than I do?" she retorted.

"I do now," he said, the haunted look in his eyes taking the bite out of his words.

If my expression was anything like Abby's, then it was full of sympathy. I was thinking about how he lost his mom and his brother, his twin. Since I didn't have a sibling, I could only imagine the depth of his grief.

He responded to our compassion with a sneer. "How lame is this party going to be? Let me guess, you invited all your loser friends, and you don't even have any alcohol to make them tolerable."

"You don't need any alcohol," Abby snapped at him. "You're mean enough without it."

She averted her gaze from him, and I knew she was thinking about her biological dad.

I wanted to comfort her, but I knew that she wouldn't want me to do it in front of Devon. I settled for glaring at him instead.

He was too perceptive though, because he glanced from her to me and back again before tilting his head as he regarded her. "You've been hurt by a mean drunk."

"Not me," she said. "He hurt my mom."

Her mouth dropped open in disbelief that she had told him that. I was just as shocked as she was, because she never talked about that with anyone.

He nodded, like he expected that. "Dads can be assholes."

"He's not my dad," she insisted, automatically rejecting him like she had since he broke her mom's rib when she was seven. "He's just a sperm donor. My real dad is great."

He nodded again. "Wish I could trade mine in too."

She looked at him with so much understanding and acceptance that I choked up with emotion for both of them.

It made Devon uncomfortable, and he fell back into what I

now knew was his signature defense mechanism. "Are we doing this or what?" he snapped.

Abby had apparently figured him out too. "Sorry we kept you waiting, your highness," she shot back.

He smirked at her. "As long as you know your place, peon."

She smirked back before turning to me. "Remember to act surprised," she reminded me.

"I will," I assured her.

She strode down the driveway toward her house, and we followed her. Unlocking her front door, she ushered me inside. I had only taken a couple of steps in when someone yelled, "Surprise!"

That was followed by a chorus of voices yelling, "Surprise!"

I saw people springing up from behind the couch and the recliners. "Oh my gosh!" I exclaimed. "I can't believe you guys did this!"

They all stared at me. After a beat, Sarah demanded, "Who told you?" She slid an accusing look toward Abby, who had walked up to stand beside me.

"I did," Devon declared as he glided to a stop beside me on my other side.

There was total silence as everyone gaped at him with their mouths open. To say that his presence here was unexpected was an understatement. He had spent the last year and a half being completely antisocial. Even when he did attend parties during those few months sophomore year, they were thrown by the most popular people from our school. We were far from that crowd. Although we weren't exactly outcasts, we were way under the radar of anyone he had ever associated with before. And if those people were the elite, he surpassed them. His family was wealthier and more distinguished than anyone else's in our town. It was the equivalent of having a celebrity in our midst.

Nobody knew how to act around him, so I took the lead. "Hey, guys, this is Devon. Devon, these are my friends."

"Hi," he said.

"Hi," they all replied in unison.

It was still extremely awkward after that, so Abby announced, "We have cake!"

I gave her a look, but she was too busy being the bright, happy hostess to notice it. "In the dining room, guys. Cake for everyone!"

She led the way, and everyone followed her while I slid a glance toward Devon. He was trying to suppress a smirk, but he lost the battle when his gaze met mine.

"I heard a rumor that there's cake," he deadpanned.

I rolled my eyes at him. "This way, smartass."

It was only when I turned my back to him and began leading him to the dining room that I was struck by the surreal realization that we had just bantered like we were friends. For a moment there, I actually forgot who he was, and it had felt natural and easy.

The traitorous thought crept into my mind. *Like it never felt with Matt.*

I tried to banish it, but it lingered. Despite his easygoing manner, I didn't feel completely at ease with him. There was a barrier between us that I couldn't breach. Maybe it was my insecurity about fitting in with him and his friends.

Devon had no friends. He was a total loner. It was by choice, but it still made me relate to him. Because I felt disconnected from my friends. A pang of guilt over that thought sliced through me, but it was the truth. Although they sympathized, they didn't know how I felt. While I couldn't pretend to know exactly how Devon felt after losing people he was so close to, I related more to him than I did to anyone else—even my best friend since kindergarten.

In an effort to dispel those unbidden thoughts, I focused my attention on her with renewed appreciation. Abby had planned this surprise party for me in an effort to cheer me up. I saw that she even got me two cakes, because she knew my preference for white cake. I assumed that the other one was chocolate to suit the tastes of the majority of the people here. That one was larger, but both were decorated with pink flowers made out of frosting. The smaller one had *Happy Birthday Hazel* written on it, and it had metallic pink one and eight number candles on it, making it clear that this was my eighteenth birthday.

"Guess you like pink," Devon muttered.

It sounded like criticism, and I flushed in embarrassment before bristling defiantly. "So, what if I like pink?" I demanded before I even realized that I was speaking. "Not everyone can be as cool as you, Lord Vader."

His dark gaze scrutinized me. "Lord Vader?"

Wishful thinking gave me hope that he didn't know who I was referring to. I was aware that it was a futile hope, but Abby dashed it completely when she explained, "It's from Star Wars. You know, Darth Vader?" She tilted her head at him. "I can kind of see it with you wearing black all the time and having that deep voice. Not as deep as James Earl Jones, but still. And you always seemed kind of intimidating, but I guess you really aren't."

She smirked at him. "Plus, you're as hot as Anakin. At least some people think so." She then directed her smirk at me, making it obvious that she was referring to me, although I knew that she thought she was being sly and secretive.

My face heated, making it even more apparent. Fortunately, Sarah intervened to save me from total humiliation. "Okay, who wants chocolate cake?"

It worked to break the awkward tension, as several people called out, "Me!"

"We have to sing Happy Birthday first," Abby protested.

"Please don't," I pleaded, wanting to avoid as much of the spotlight as possible.

"How about you just blow out your candles," Sarah suggested, heading off Abby's objections.

"Yes," I agreed quickly, stepping toward the cake to get it done. "Where's the lighter?"

"I'll do it," Abby grumbled.

I was preparing to blow the candles out as soon as she lit them, but her admonishment made me pause. "Make a wish," she insisted.

I stared at the twin flames atop the metallic pink candles, and I was transported to a happier time when I still believed in fairy-tales. The wish in my heart then was simple, and it slipped into my mind with its pure, uncomplicated clarity. *True love. I wish for true love.*

I blew out the candles with one big breath, and it felt magical. Until the sound of clapping jolted me back to reality. I wasn't ten years old and still believing in someday. I was eighteen, now legally an adult, and I knew better than to believe in birthday wishes. I never got the pony I wished for when I was six.

"I did, but I can't ride him anymore."

I realized two things in that moment: I had spoken my thought about the pony aloud, and Devon had just revealed something about himself to me—voluntarily.

I wanted to fist pump in victory, but I knew that I couldn't make a big deal about it, or he'd clam up and never tell me anything again. "What's his name?" I asked, as casual as can be.

"Midnight," he answered. "Not original, since his coat is black, but I was eight." He gave me a wry smile.

"I love that name," I told him truthfully. "So much better than Black Beauty, but I really loved that book when I was a kid. My mom passed it down to me. It was her favorite when she was growing up. She used to read it to me before I could read it myself. It's what started my obsession with horses."

"How often do you ride?" he asked.

I had to suppress a smile, because I was having a conversation with Devon. I was actually having a conversation with him! "I got to ride a pony once at a fair," I told him. "It was the highlight of my childhood." I did smile then, remembering how excited and happy I looked in that picture.

Devon frowned. "You've never been riding?"

"Only that pony at the fair."

He scoffed. "That's a trot around a track. That's not real riding."

I shrugged. "It was good enough for me. My seven-year-old heart was satisfied."

"Tomorrow," he declared. "I'll take you to my stables. It'll be my gift to you."

I gaped at him. Did he just offer to take me horseback riding?

"Okay," Abby said, "I know you want white cake, Hazel. What about you, Devon?"

"White," he answered her, breaking eye contact with me to glance at her.

Her face registered surprise. "You too? I thought Hazel was the only person who would pass up chocolate cake." She smirked. "You must be twins."

She stilled, her eyes going wide. "I'm so sorry! I wasn't thinking."

"It's okay," he assured her. "My twin would have gladly pawned me off on Hazel."

She smiled weakly, but I could tell that she was still upset with herself. Her movements were stiff as she removed the candles and began to cut the cake.

"I would have given you right back to him," I teased, trying to alleviate the awkwardness.

"Here's your inferior cake," Abby said brightly as she handed me a piece on a paper plate. It was obvious her forced cheerfulness was a tactic to move past the reminder of Devon's deceased twin. "Sorry, Devon, the birthday girl gets the first piece."

That's when I remembered that Devon and I were born on the same day. Which meant...

It was his birthday too.

I was still processing that as my gaze traveled toward him. Abby carried on, oblivious. I had never told her that tidbit that I discovered while I was obsessively gleaning any information I could about him back in freshman year at the height of my crush on him. "Here you go," she said as she handed him the plate with his piece of cake and patted his other arm.

As she was pulling back, he grabbed her hand with his free one, making her gasp in surprise. She stared at him before shifting her gaze to me, obviously seeking guidance as he continued to hold her hand. Before I could think of what to say or do, he ended their strange encounter by finally letting go of her hand.

Abruptly, he set the plate she just gave him on the table. "I have to make a phone call," he said and maneuvered his way out of the room.

"What was that?" Abby asked me.

I was just as mystified as she was. "I have no idea."

Sarah joined us and lowered her voice so the rest of our friends wouldn't hear. "Why was Devon holding your hand?" she questioned Abby. "Did he ask you out?"

"No," Abby replied. "I don't know what that was about. He didn't say anything, except that he has to go make a phone call."

Sarah looked just as confused as the two of us, but then she shrugged. "Whatever. It's just cool that you got him to come to Hazel's party. Remember when she used to have a crush on him?"

"Shh!" I instantly shushed her as I darted a panicked glance at our friends, who were gathered at the other end of the table where the chocolate cake was. They were eating and talking, and I was relieved that they were currently not paying attention to us.

"Wait," Sarah said slowly, her eyes widening as she stared at me. "Do you still have a crush on him?"

"Shut up!" I hissed at her.

"Oh my God, you do!"

"He's coming back," Abby said urgently.

Sarah went silent, and the three of us stood there like statues as Devon came up to us. He scrutinized us. "What's wrong?"

"Nothing!" we all denied in unison.

Yeah, that wasn't suspicious. Trying to deflect, I turned it around on him. "Is everything okay with you? Your phone call... uh, nothing's wrong I hope."

He looked at Abby before replying to me. "I'm fine."

A beat passed, during which his gaze drifted to Abby again. "Uh, aren't you going to eat your cake?" she asked him.

He glanced at it and then at the uneaten piece I was still holding. "Aren't you going to eat yours?" he asked me.

"Yeah," I said, picking up the plastic fork to lift a bite to my mouth. "Somebody has to eat this delicious cake, right?" I put the forkful in my mouth and savored the combination of moist cake and the rich sweetness of the frosting. "It's good," I told him, but his eyes were on Abby.

"Truth or dare!" someone yelled, drawing our attention to him.

Kyle bounded over to us as I rolled my eyes. "We're not playing truth or dare," I insisted.

He grinned at me. "Afraid you'll lose control if you kiss me again?"

I glared at him, still feeling cheated that he stole my first kiss.

"She had a crush on this loser in middle school," he told Devon.

"Shut up!" I exclaimed.

"She wanted him to be her first kiss," he continued, "but I ruined that for him. I dared her to kiss me, and she couldn't chicken out in front of him, so she did it."

"Oh my God, shut up!" I yelled. "That was forever ago."

"She's been in love with me ever since," he said and smirked.

"You are the worst," I retorted and turned on Abby. "Why did you invite him? You know I can't stand him."

"You love me," Kyle insisted.

Abby was laughing at our bickering, like she always did. In the next instant, she collapsed. Devon shot toward her, but she was on the floor before he could reach her. The rest of us were still standing motionless in shock.

Kyle lurched out of his paralysis and rushed to fall to his knees beside her. "Abby!" he yelled in panic and shook her arm, trying to wake her.

My vocal cords unfroze, and I exclaimed, "Abby!"

Sarah shouted, "Someone call 911!"

"They're on their way," Devon said.

"What happened?" someone asked.

"She fainted," someone else replied.

"Too much running," Emily said. "I told her cross country would be too much. She should have joined track instead."

Emily didn't sound as concerned as the rest of us. Not because she didn't care, but because she was a total optimist. Her mind never went to the worst-case scenario, and she always thought that everything would work out okay.

Kyle, on the other hand, looked devastated. "Abby," he cried out in anguish as he cradled her head on his lap. "Please wake up."

"I don't think he was supposed to move her," a girl said anxiously.

"It's okay," Emily told her. "She just fainted. She's not injured or anything."

I was only listening to their voices, because I hadn't taken my eyes off Abby. She was unresponsive, so how Emily could assume anything about her condition was beyond me. The wail of a siren was startling but so very welcome.

"I'll let them in!" I exclaimed and rushed to open the front door.

I waited anxiously as the sound of the siren got louder, and I was filled with relief when I spotted the ambulance. As it pulled into the driveway, I heard adult voices behind me.

"What's happened?" a man's voice asked.

"Abby!" a woman screamed.

Oh crap, I had forgotten about Abby's parents! They must have heard the siren and come downstairs to investigate. Abby had told me that they were going to be watching TV in their bedroom.

I let the paramedics in, and they took charge of the situation. The rest of us stood back and watched anxiously. When they rushed her out on a stretcher, her parents left with them, unaware of anything else.

While we all remained shell-shocked, Devon took control in a calm but firm voice. "Everyone has to leave. We can't stay here when they're not home."

His words roused me. "He's right. We have to go."

Kyle was already heading toward the door before I finished speaking. "I'm going to the hospital."

"Me too. I have to know if she's okay," Sarah said, rushing after him.

There were murmurs of agreement, and our small group of friends was soon gone, leaving me behind with Devon and Emily. She was the one who remembered to put the leftover cake into containers so that it wouldn't dry out. I dumped the partially consumed beverages down the kitchen sink and threw away the pink solo cups, getting choked up while thinking of Abby getting them especially for me.

"She'll be okay," Emily said.

I didn't have much faith in her optimism right then. After what happened to Matt, I knew that things didn't always turn out okay. Before that, I never would have imagined that any of my friends could die. Now I was worried that it was a very real possibility. My heart seized at the thought of Abby dying.

"I'll drive you to the hospital," Devon offered.

I saw Emily watching us curiously, but I didn't care about appearances right then. It was probably rude to accept his offer without considering her, but she hadn't offered me a ride in her car. Knowing her, she just didn't want to get in the way of me going with Devon. Most likely, she was under the delusion that he was interested in me.

I didn't dwell on any of that as I replied, "That would be great, thanks."

"I'll meet you there," Emily said, confirming my suspicions.

We left the house, and I made sure to lock the door. Melancholy overwhelmed me for a moment over the abrupt end of the party I hadn't wanted. What I wouldn't have given now for it to have continued as Abby planned, even if I had to suffer through a stupid game of truth or dare.

I was desperately hoping that Abby would be okay, but Devon offered me no false assurances. He drove in silence, reminding me of when he gave me a ride home the day that Matt died. This time, however, he was the one who had called 911 for Abby—before she collapsed.

The realization was swift and shocking.

I recalled him leaving the room to make a phone call. I also remembered how he kept watching Abby afterwards. Like maybe he knew something was going to happen.

Again.

"How did you know?" I asked in amazement.

He glanced at me, his gaze wary as it met my awed one. "I didn't."

"You called 911 before she fainted," I said. "That's why the ambulance got there so fast." That realization made me grateful to him, because he got her help as soon as possible.

His eyes were back on the road, and he said nothing.

I had so many questions, but his denial made it obvious that he wouldn't answer them. I didn't understand why he was hiding his ability, but I decided to respect his decision. Still, questions persisted in my mind. How did it work? Why did he know about me and Abby, but not about Matt?

I replayed everything that had just happened, looking for clues. Abby gave him the piece of cake, and then he set it down without eating it and excused himself to go make a phone call. No, there was something else that happened before that. It was easy to remember since it was so unexpected and surprising. He grabbed her hand.

That memory was suddenly interposed with the one of him grabbing my arms to steady me after I almost fell on him. He touched both me and Abby. But he didn't touch Matt.

"It works through touch?" I blurted.

My gaze shot toward him for confirmation, but he continued to stare silently out the windshield. I did notice that his jaw was clenched, and his posture was rigid. He obviously didn't like that I had figured it out.

"I won't tell anyone," I assured him. "I swear."

He gave no indication of whether he believed me or not, and he dropped me off at the hospital without another word. He just stopped the truck in front of the entrance and gave me a flat look. I could read it clearly. It said *get out*.

"Thank you for driving me," I told him politely anyway.

When he didn't respond, I opened the door and lowered myself out of his truck. As soon as I shut the door, he pulled away. Not fast like he was mad, but easily and without a parting glance at me—like he didn't care.

It was his usual demeanor, but I had seen past it now. This cool, aloof guy did care. He wouldn't have saved my life if he didn't. And Abby's. At least I hoped she was alive. My concern for my best friend propelled me into the hospital, and thoughts of Devon faded into the background.

CHAPTER 4

I was stunned to discover that my seventeen-year-old best friend had gone into sudden cardiac arrest. Her parents were so grateful to me once I finally found them. With tears in their eyes, they told me that Abby might have died if the ambulance hadn't arrived when it did. They thanked me for calling 911 so promptly. I informed them that it wasn't me but Devon Culver who called. Surprise registered on their faces. They obviously recognized the name due to the status of his family. They didn't ask any questions though and simply said that they would have to thank him.

No one but family was allowed to see Abby, so her parents thanked all her friends who were gathered in the waiting room and urged us to go home, assuring us that she would be okay. We remained and talked for a while after they left us. Sarah spouted off facts about sudden cardiac arrest she had looked up.

"I've heard of it happening to athletes," she said, "but I always thought it was from heatstroke. It says here though that about two thousand young people under the age of twenty-five die from it every year, and most of them seem perfectly healthy." She shuddered as she clutched her phone. "Abby was so lucky to survive."

Emily looked shell-shocked by how close Abby came to dying. I had never seen her like that, and I felt bad that this had blindsided her so badly. "You were right," I told her, trying to get her back to her normal, optimistic self. "She's okay, just like you said."

She stared at me. "She almost died."

"But she didn't," I stated firmly, taking charge for her sake. "C'mon, let's go home. We can't do anything else here tonight."

I took her hand, and she went with me, seemingly on automatic pilot. Kyle was in a similar state, but he walked with us on his own. Despite how much he loved to mess with me about being my first kiss, I had seen how he looked at Abby. I had known for a long time that he was in love with her. I even confronted him about it one time, but he denied it.

I heard our other friends talking as they trailed behind us. The three of us were completely silent though. They caught up to us in the parking lot, and Sarah spoke for them as she invited us to go out to eat with them. They were all in a celebratory mood due to the good news about Abby being okay and on the road to recovery. My two companions and I were still stuck on the fact that she almost died, however. I spoke for us as I declined the invitation and said that we were tired and wanted to go home.

"But it's your birthday," Sarah protested.

"And we had cake and a party," I replied, but I ruined my matter-of-fact tone with a wince at the thought of how it had ended.

Sarah saw it and retorted, "And it was ruined! Come out with us, and—"

"It was saved," I interjected, interrupting her.

My mind flashed to who saved it. To the person who saved Abby. "It's Devon's birthday too," I blurted without meaning to.

Sarah's mouth dropped open in surprise. "It is?"

"Yeah, but don't make a big deal about it," I pleaded, knowing that it was a mistake to tell anyone. With how private he was, it was a given that he wouldn't appreciate it.

The sympathy in her eyes didn't bode well. "I mean it," I told her sternly. "He doesn't want to celebrate his birthday." In desperation to get my point across, I leaned in and said quietly into her ear, "It's his twin's birthday too."

Comprehension showed in her expression when I pulled back. I saw that I could trust her not to make any well-meaning gestures in honor of Devon's birthday, since she didn't want to trigger painful memories of his deceased brother. If she knew about how he saved Abby's life, I wouldn't be able to stop her from doing something to thank him. That was part of the reason that I kept it to myself.

I also didn't know if she would believe me. But it was more than that. I already felt like I had betrayed Devon just by telling her that it was his birthday. That was ridiculous, of course, but he seemed to have infected me with his secretive demeanor. I was cautious about revealing too much.

I also wanted to prove to him that I could be trusted. Because I was now hoping that we could become friends. That wasn't as farfetched as it once was. The fact that he came to my birthday party proved that it was a possibility. I was no longer obsessed with him in a romantic way, at least. Ever since Matt died, romance hadn't been on my mind—despite me making that wish for true love. That was just a lovely dream for the future. Hopefully it would happen sometime when I was in my twenties.

Right then I was focused on my friends. Kyle and Emily also declined the invitation to go out to eat, and we parted ways with Sarah and the others. "Are you okay to drive?" I asked Kyle.

He took a deep breath and expelled it before speaking. "Yeah, I'm okay now that I know she's okay. It's a miracle that I made it here without crashing the car though. I was speeding like that was going to save her." He shook his head and sighed heavily. "That was the worst feeling."

He fixed his gaze on me. "I'm sorry, Hazel. I didn't know how you felt. Of course, I felt bad for you, but I didn't really know how horrible it was for you to lose Matt. Not until I almost lost Abby."

Guilt hit me in the gut, because I had hardly been thinking about Matt at all today. What kind of person was I that I could so easily be distracted by a boy and a party? Yes, the boy had top billing over the party, and I was more intrigued by him than ever.

"I know you love Abby," I said, deflecting from commenting on Matt.

"I do," he said to my surprise. He had always denied it before. "I'm going to tell her when she's better."

"Oh," I responded, not knowing what to say.

He gave me a weary smile. "Okay, I'm tired now. I've gotta go home and crash. See you tomorrow?"

"Yeah," I agreed.

He walked off, and I looked at Emily. She was standing there looking just as out of it as she was in the waiting room. She definitely didn't seem capable of driving, so I asked for her keys. When she handed them over without question or comment, I knew that she was running on autopilot. Luckily, she was able to direct me to where she parked her car, and I drove her home.

I saw her to her door and handed her back her keys. After saying goodnight to her, I debated whether to walk home. Emily's house was only two blocks away from mine, but I was spooked by the thought of walking home in the dark. I was too aware right now of how vulnerable I was. If Abby could be in danger at a birthday party, then how much more dangerous was it for me to be alone outside in the dark? For a moment, I wished that Devon was here, because I felt safe with him.

That was an unexpected realization, but I pushed it to the back of my mind along with all the other discoveries I had made about him today. I had a lot to think about—after I got home. I pulled out my phone and called my mom to come pick me up. I gave her a brief explanation about what happened to Abby, and about how I had to drive Emily home due to her being in shock.

Mom exclaimed in dismay over all the events of the evening, but I was starting to feel strangely numb. She was all concerned when she arrived, but I was calm as I got in the car. The distance from my emotions had me telling her about Devon calling 911 before Abby showed any signs of anything being wrong with her.

Mom was quiet for a moment, and I thought she didn't believe me. Then she stunned me when she said, "My grandmother knew things before they happened."

This cut through my numbness. "What?" I exclaimed.

She made the turn into our driveway. Our short journey was already at an end, but our conversation wasn't. She faced me and said, "When I was eight, she told my mother not to go on our annual family vacation. She said that disaster awaited us. My mother didn't listen, and we got into a car accident. My parents both ended up in the hospital with broken bones. My brother and I were in the backseat, and we were lucky enough to be spared injury."

"That's amazing!" I responded excitedly. "We have a psychic in the family? How did I not know this?"

Mom sighed. "My mother distanced herself from her, because she was embarrassed by her. Grandma was a bit of a local celebrity. She would do readings for people, telling them their fortunes. People from all the surrounding towns would seek her out too, since she was known to be so good at her predictions."

"My great-grandma was a fortune teller?" I asked in wonder.

Mom smiled sadly. "It's too bad she didn't live long enough to meet you. She knew about you long before that though, because she told me when I was ten years old that my daughter would be her namesake. That was well before I knew what a namesake was. We stayed with her while our parents were in the hospital, and I got to spend time with her for the first time. She also took care of all of us after my parents went home with casts. My mom had a broken arm, and my dad had a broken leg, so they couldn't refuse her help."

"Why wouldn't they want her help?" I questioned in confusion.

Mom shook her head and rolled her eyes. "Because they were respectable people. They didn't want to be tainted by association with a tacky fortune teller."

"But we live in Salem," I said. "If there's anywhere that having a psychic relative is cool, it's here. We have a witch museum for goodness' sake."

Mom shrugged. "I guess my mother always wanted a different life. She married a lawyer, and she put me in ballet lessons. She made my brother learn to play the piano, even though all he cared about was sports."

My uncle was a gym teacher at our high school and the football coach, so that didn't surprise me. I snickered at the thought of him being forced to play piano.

Mom pinpointed the source of my amusement. "He's actually pretty good," she told me. "Certainly not a virtuoso by any means, but not terrible either. He'd never admit it, but I think it gave him a creative outlet that he enjoyed. Why else would he have a piano in his house?"

"I thought that was for Aunt Jill," I said.

"She plays also," Mom acknowledged, "but your uncle Tom likes to play it too."

I was astonished by this revelation. "I never would have imagined him playing the piano," I admitted. "He's such a jock. But I can totally see you taking ballet. No wonder you have such grace and poise. Couldn't you have passed a little of it down to me?" I joked.

"I tried putting you in ballet when you were four, but you didn't pay any attention to the teacher. You just talked to the ghost girl."

I startled at this. "The ghost girl?"

Mom nodded. "It was an invisible girl only you could see. You told me that her name was Svetlana."

I shrugged. "She was obviously an imaginary friend."

"And you came up with the name Svetlana?" she countered. "You were four years old, Hazel. It wasn't like we knew anybody with that name. So, I looked into it, and I found out that there was a little girl named Svetlana who used to take ballet at that studio. She disappeared one day while at the lake with her family."

"That's so sad," I said, caught up in the story now. "Did they ever find out what happened to her?"

Mom nodded. "You told me where to find her."

I gaped at her. "I...what?"

"I got creeped out and took you out of ballet. But one Saturday morning you told me that Svetlana wanted to show you something at the lake." She gazed somberly at me. "You said that our neighbor was going out on his boat, and that she wanted us to go with him. I had a feeling she'd lead you to where her body was. I admit that I was just hoping she'd go away after that, which was really the only reason I bothered Mr. Daniels to take us with him. I could tell that he didn't really want to, but he was too polite to say no."

"How come I don't remember any of this?" I asked in dismay.

"You were only four," she reminded me. "Most people don't remember anything from that age."

She was right, because my first memory was of meeting Abby in kindergarten. "So, Mr. Daniels took us out on his boat," I prompted, wanting her to continue.

"Yes," she said. "Your dad was away on a business trip, so it was just you and me and Mr. Daniels. When you pointed out toward the middle of the lake and said that Svetlana wanted us to go there, he looked spooked, but he followed your directions. He dropped anchor where you told him to stop, and we all just looked down into the water for a moment. He was the one who called the police. While we waited, he told me that he had helped search for Svetlana when she went missing."

She expelled a breath. "When you said to him that she knows, and she says thank you, his face..."

She trailed off and shook her head before fixing an emotional gaze on me. "He looked so touched. I could tell that he believed you. I did too, and I asked you what happened to her. You said that she went under the water and couldn't get out."

She sighed. "From what I was able to piece together, her family didn't see her go back into the water after they got out to dry off. She must have drowned before they noticed she was gone."

"How awful," I said with a shudder, picturing the scene.

"It was," Mom agreed. "I can't imagine you just being gone like that." Her eyes filled with tears. "You almost were."

I knew she was thinking about what would have happened if I was in the car with Matt, but I was way too intrigued with Svetlana's story to dwell on that. "So, they found her body in the lake?"

As I'd hoped, Mom was drawn back into telling the rest of the tale. "Yes," she answered. "Luckily, the police chief was Mr. Daniels's cousin, because I doubt they would have listened to us otherwise. Mr. Daniels still lied and told them that I was the one with the premonition about where to find Svetlana's body, since they weren't likely to take a four-year-old seriously. The police chief was extremely skeptical about me as well, but he sent divers down to look anyway, and they found her right where you said she was. Her family finally got closure after three years."

"Three years!" I exclaimed. "How could she be down there that long? Wouldn't she have floated to the surface way before that?"

"I would have thought so too," Mom said. "But, apparently, that tends to happen more in warmer, shallower lakes. Since ours is deep and cold, a body is more likely to sink to the bottom and stay fairly preserved down there."

That thought crept me out as I thought about all the times I had gone swimming while completely unaware that there could be dead bodies beneath me. A chill went down my spine, and I hurried on from that topic. "So, did she move on after that?" I asked, remembering the movie, Ghost.

"I think so," Mom answered. "You never mentioned her again after that."

"But how could I just forget about her?" I questioned in dismay. "I saw a ghost!"

"You didn't think of her that way," Mom said. "To you, she was like anyone else you talked to. Small children are much more accepting of the impossible. You believed in Santa Clause and fairies and unicorns, after all. Also, your attention span was short. So, when you didn't see her anymore, she must have faded from your mind."

"Do you remember her last name?" I queried. "I want to see if I can find a picture of her."

Mom pulled out her phone and tapped on it for a while

before handing it to me. I saw an adorable little blonde girl with blue eyes, and my heart filled with sadness for the loss of a life so young. Yet nothing about her was familiar to me. I was hoping that her picture would trigger a memory, but I didn't remember her at all. It was disconcerting not to have any recollection of this.

Of course, I didn't remember preschool either, regardless of the pictures of me with my class. That didn't trouble me though, maybe because it was so ordinary. Seeing a ghost, however—that seemed like something that should be unforgettable.

"Why didn't you ever tell me any of this before?" I complained.

Mom sighed. "Because you never mentioned it, and I thought it was best to just let it go. At first, I kept expecting you to see more ghosts or predict the future like my Grandma Hazel. I thought maybe you'd inherited her abilities, but it was apparently a onetime thing for you."

"How could it only happen one time?" I demanded. "Either I'm psychic or I'm not."

"I was wondering that myself," she said. "I looked into psychic abilities, and I discovered that some people think we all have them. It's just that most people can't tap into them. So, what I think is that you were able to tap into them that one time. Probably because you were so little, and your mind was so open. You didn't have doubt and skepticism blocking you. Or," she added with a wry smile, "maybe Svetlana was the only ghost around here. Fortunately, we don't have a lot of tragedy happening in this town."

That statement triggered us both to think about Matt's tragic accident. I could see it in her pained expression. "I'm sorry," she said. "I wasn't thinking."

"It's okay," I told her. "I wasn't thinking about him either."

That sounded really bad, and I cringed and admitted, "I hardly thought about him at all today."

She donned that *I'm-imparting-words-of-wisdom* mom expression. It was serious but sympathetic. "You don't have to grieve every day. In fact, you don't have to grieve at all anymore if you've been able to move on. There is no set grieving time that everyone has to follow. For some people it's short, and for other people it lasts for years. Neither one is wrong. It's a very personal thing. But I'm glad you were able to forget about it today and enjoy your birthday. At least until..."

She expelled a breath. "I'm so glad that Abby is okay."

"Me too," I agreed. "Thanks to Devon." I sighed and said, "Today is his birthday too."

Mom startled at this. "It is?"

"Yeah, but he never said anything. I didn't remember until we were having cake. But then I realized that it's his twin's birthday too, so maybe that's why he didn't want to talk about it?"

"Maybe," she agreed, looking troubled.

I wondered if she was having the same thoughts I was. "Mom, do you think that..."

I took a breath and expelled my question. "Do you think his family celebrates his birthday?"

"Well, of course," she responded, but her expression became unsure after she said it. "I mean, I know it would be difficult with what happened to their other child, but surely..."

She trailed off, wavering from reassuring me. Suddenly, there was a determined look on her face. "Invite him over for cake on Saturday."

"Mom," I protested, "you can't have a birthday party for him. That will just be weird. Besides, his family might have had one for him. Or maybe they're having one this weekend."

"It won't be a birthday party," she said. "It will be a party in honor of him saving Abby's life."

I shook my head. "He did that in secret. He doesn't want anyone knowing about his premonitions. He definitely wouldn't be happy about me telling you."

"Well, then, we can just say it's in honor of his quick thinking in calling 911. I won't let on that I know anything beyond that."

I considered this, feeling torn about it. I would have loved to have him over and spend more time with him, but I was afraid that he'd reject my invitation. I had been cut by his rejection before, and it wasn't something that I ever wanted to experience again. Yet the fact that he came to my party on his birthday made me suspect that there was no celebration for him. That thought hurt my heart.

So, I swallowed my pride the next day at school as I approached him at his locker and blurted, "My mom wants you to come over tomorrow."

His dark eyes widened in surprise. "What?"

I had managed to catch him off guard, and I went with it. "Yeah, she says that you have to ask her for my hand in marriage before we can wed." I rolled my eyes. "It's so 1800's."

My heart started pounding a million miles a minute. Why had I said that? I was trying to be sarcastic and funny, but that was just weird.

To my utter astonishment, he played along. He smirked and then said, "If those are the rules, then I guess I have to follow them."

I knew that my eyes must be as big as saucers. "You do?"

His smirk softened into warm amusement. "Yeah."

"Uh, okay," I responded, abandoning the banter in my nervousness. "Is two o'clock tomorrow okay?"

His gaze traveled down the length of me before returning to my face. He looked directly into my eyes as he said, "Yes."

It was one word, but it seemed to convey so many things. I sensed an underlying meaning to his response, but I couldn't unravel it. All I knew was that it had unnerved me completely. "See you then," was all I managed before fleeing.

I was walking as quickly as I could without running, but it wasn't just from the adrenaline rush of having done this incredibly nerve-wracking thing. Giddiness was also propelling my feet. *He said yes! He wants to come over and spend time with me!*

Within a short time, my burst of excitement made me feel guilty. Because my best friend was in the hospital, and I was here all giddy over a guy. And my boyfriend was dead.

That guilt hit me harder. Because Matt was not going to recover and come home. That made it even more unfair that I was experiencing any sort of happiness at all. It was unfair that I was alive and he was dead. Why wasn't he saved too?

The answer crept into my mind. Because Devon didn't touch him. It was such a bizarre thing to make the difference between life and death. If I hadn't bumped into Devon in the hallway at school, he wouldn't have known I was in danger, and I would have ridden home in Matt's car and died in the crash with him. And if Devon hadn't come to my birthday party, Abby wouldn't have made physical contact with him, and she would have died before help could arrive. Because nobody would have known that anything was wrong until she collapsed. Devon was the only one who knew.

He was the only one who knew when something bad was going to happen. Which made me wonder why he couldn't foresee his own accident—and his mom and brother's death.

Once that thought got into my head, it wouldn't let go. Had he just not touched his mom or his brother that day?

I imagined if I had that power that I'd want to touch my family every day to make sure they weren't in danger. I could easily picture myself getting paranoid about it and going overboard. Maybe he wanted to avoid becoming obsessive about it and restrained himself from touching them more than normal. Still, it seemed weird to me that he wouldn't have some kind of premonition about himself. Would touching his own arm work?

I had so many crazy questions that I knew I wouldn't ever dare to ask him. The fact that he was talking to me at all was enough of a miracle. Having him come over to my house was beyond my wildest dreams. I wasn't going to risk driving him away with questions he didn't want to answer.

So, I focused on Abby's situation and went to the hospital after school. To my happy surprise, I was allowed to see her. She was conscious and alert, and that brought tears of relief to my eyes. Stress I didn't know I was carrying drained out of me.

"Hazel," she said, greeting me with a smile. "Some party, huh?"

I choked out a laugh. "Yeah, it was killer."

I winced right after I said it, but Abby grinned. "That's the perfect way to describe it."

It was a term my mom occasionally used when she seemed to fall back into excited teenage girl mode, and it was the only slang word from her time I thought sounded cool, even though I would never tell her that. In this instance though, it was a little too close to what almost happened.

I mentally shook it off and asked, "What happened? Do the doctors know?"

"Yeah, it turns out that my septum is too thick. That's the wall between heart chambers. They're going to try medication first. If that doesn't work, they'll have to do surgery."

She saw my distress over this news and said, "Hey, I'm lucky. They got me to the hospital in time to save me. I almost..."

Despite having just been amused over my slang use of the word killer, she couldn't say died. She almost died.

And she would have if Devon hadn't sensed it and called 911 before she even showed any symptoms of anything being wrong. I was so tempted to tell her everything right then, but something held me back.

Devon. He was so secretive about his ability. It felt like it would be a betrayal to tell his secret to anyone else.

So, instead, I revealed my own hitherto unknown ability as I launched into the story my mom told me about my connection to the dead girl, Svetlana.

Abby's eyes were wide when I finished. "You see dead people."

I laughed, recalling the line from the movie she was paraphrasing. "Apparently, I did once."

"But why did it stop?" she questioned in confusion. "The kid in the movie saw a bunch of dead people."

I shuddered at the thought. "Thank God I didn't. Luckily, I seem to have grown out of it and forgotten that it ever happened."

She gave me a speculative look. "But it's still in you. It might be buried deep inside, but if you could do it once, you probably could again if you tried hard enough."

The thought of seeing another dead person made me uneasy. "But why would I want to?"

She fixed a look on me. "Because you helped that girl find peace. Why wouldn't you want to help more people?"

"Uh, because it's creepy," I replied, even as her question was making me feel guilty. Of course, I wanted to help people if I could.

"You weren't creeped out when you were a kid," she pointed out.

"That's because I didn't know I was talking to a dead person," I retorted.

"Exactly," she said with satisfaction. "Which means that she didn't look or act creepy. It's not like the ghosts in that movie at all. She was like a regular girl. Like I would have been if I had died."

I recoiled at the mere thought, but she pressed on. "You would have helped me if I came to you, right?"

"Yeah," I said, "but I don't even want to think about that happening to you."

"Me either," she admitted. "But what if I'm doomed now? Like in those Final Destination movies."

"You're not," I assured her. "Devon saved me, and I'm still here."

Her eyes widened. "That's right! He kept you from going home with Matt."

I took a breath and blurted, "And he called 911 before you fainted."

Her eyes were as big as saucers now. "He's psychic?"

I was instantly regretting revealing his secret. It felt like I had betrayed his trust—already. When he was only just beginning to share any part of himself with me. "Don't tell anyone!" I pleaded.

"I won't," she promised. "But tell me everything."

I hesitated.

"C'mon, Hazel," she coaxed. "I swear I won't tell anyone. You know you can trust me."

I did trust her. She was my best friend, and the urge to confide in her overrode my hesitation. Still, I held back the detail about touch being the trigger for Devon's psychic ability. I wanted to keep my promise to him, even if it was only a small part of it.

When I was done, she stared at me in wonder. "He saved us," she marveled. "He saved both of us."

That stunned me. I hadn't thought of it that way, but she was right. Devon had saved both me and my best friend. Something about that seemed significant. What were the chances that this aloof boy, who had previously had no contact with us at all, would suddenly save both of our lives on two separate occasions?

CHAPTER 5

changed outfits three times before Devon arrived. First, I put on a dress, and then realized that was too much for what was supposed to be a casual invite to my house. I then put on my usual outfit for lounging around the house—sweatpants and a t-shirt. When I looked at myself in the mirror, I knew that I had gone too far in the opposite direction. So, I changed out the sweatpants for jeans and was satisfied that I had achieved the right amount of casual while still looking presentable.

Gazing at my reflection, I took in the rosy glow of my cheeks and the excited sparkle in my eyes. I felt like I had just gotten ready for a date. I knew I shouldn't be thinking that way, but I went ahead and applied lip gloss anyway.

The moment when I opened the door to him was surreal. Devon Culver was here at my house to meet my parents and dine with us. Not even in my most romantic fantasies had I ever imagined such a scenario.

There was a look in his eyes, though, that I had never seen before. It flustered me and made my pulse race as he held eye contact with me. His gaze dropped and traveled slowly down my body until it skimmed back up to my now flushed face. His lips formed a smirk so wicked that I felt indecent just having it directed at me.

"Uh, come in," I said as my gaze skittered away from him.

He entered, maneuvering his wheelchair up the doorstep with surprising ease. Only then did I realize that he had to come up the porch steps with it, since we didn't have a ramp. It was obviously some top-of-the-line model that was specially equipped to climb stairs. Of course, with his wealth, he would have the best of anything that money could buy. Just like his truck, which he didn't have to even lift himself into.

That made me wonder how he got those fantastic arms, which rivaled those of any jock at school. He must have done some kind of weight training to have such sculpted biceps. I realized that I was staring at them and looked away in embarrassment, hoping he didn't notice.

"It's okay. You can look," he told me, dashing that hope. "I like looking at you too."

My heart seized in my chest before it began to beat wildly. Did he really just say that? The sultry look in his eyes—which I now understood was what was known as a heated look—told me that he did. It was something I had read about in books but never seen in real life. It was hot—so hot that it was making my temperature rise.

Even though it flustered me, I couldn't tear my gaze away from his. It was like he had me under some kind of spell, and only he could break it.

He did when he heard the sound of my mom's voice.

"Oh, hello," she said as she walked up to greet him. "You must be Devon. It's wonderful to meet you. I'm Hazel's mom."

He was startled, looking from her to me. However, it only took him a few seconds to school his features into a polite expression and reply to her. "It's nice to meet you too, Mrs. Guthrie."

He glanced at me, and the heat was definitely gone from his gaze now. The cold aloofness was back, and my confused heart sank with disappointment. For a moment, it had seemed like he liked me. Or at least...

I like looking at you.

The heat I had felt a moment ago resurfaced briefly at the

memory of him saying that to me. But it was quickly snuffed out as I glanced at him. I could try to convince myself that he was just hiding his attraction to me in the presence of my mom, but his indifference to me was so complete that it stung. He wasn't sneaking secret looks at me when my mom's back was turned while she led him to the dining room table. In fact, he seemed to be deliberately ignoring me.

I was proven right as he proceeded to talk to my parents without ever once speaking to me during the entire meal. Despite what she said about inviting him over for cake, my mom also cooked. Devon's focus was mostly on his food, but he engaged in conversation with them easily enough as he answered their questions and also made polite small talk like he did it every day. There was nothing awkward or hesitant about him, and no one would ever be able to tell that he had been antisocial and a complete loner for the past year and a half. He chatted so easily with my parents, like he was on their level—an equal. Like he was an adult.

Well, technically, he was. He was eighteen. So was I, but he seemed so much more grown up than me. Maybe because he'd had sex. I couldn't believe my mind just went there in the presence of my parents! My gaze darted toward my mom as my face heated in embarrassment. I was so glad that no one could hear my thoughts. I shot a look at Devon to make sure he hadn't suddenly developed that power, but he was still not sparing me a glance, so it appeared that I was in the clear.

I tried to stop observing him and ignore him like he'd been ignoring me, but my eyes were constantly drawn to him like always when he was around. I didn't understand this magnetic pull he had on me. Yes, he was gorgeous, but it always seemed like more than that. Like there was some kind of mysterious connection between us. Maybe I just needed to tell myself that in order to justify my obsession with him, because he obviously didn't feel a connection to me.

Why was he here then? Why did he accept my invitation to come over and meet my parents? And what was all that when he first arrived? The flirting and gazing into my eyes. Was it some kind of mind game? I recalled the incident in the cafeteria when he held my gaze and made me think it was a silent invitation to sit with him, until he ignored me when I approached him.

Annoyance swept over me, and I stewed in my seat until it was time to help Mom clear the dishes. Devon told her that everything was delicious and thanked her for having him over. He started to back out from the table, but she quickly stayed him.

"Hold on. We have dessert."

"Thank you, but I'm full," he replied.

"You can have a small piece," she insisted.

He relented with a polite smile. "Okay."

I got the sense that he was impatient to leave, but his expression didn't give it away. At that moment, I realized that maybe this was his allure for me. I was always wondering what was beneath the surface, what his true thoughts and feelings were.

I set the table with the dessert plates and forks, which Mom insisted on instead of paper plates and plastic forks. No doubt, she was thinking about how he grew up rich and was used to fancy place settings. Devon didn't look at me as I put the small plate down in front of him, and it further aggravated me. I slammed his dessert fork down, startling him into glancing up at me.

"Sorry," I said in an obviously fake manner. "It slipped out of my hand."

His dark eyes narrowed at me as we had a brief stare down, but Mom interrupted it when she brought out the cake. *Thank you Devon* was written on it in light blue icing. He stared at it, before raising his eyes to her.

"Your quick thinking saved Abby's life," she told him. "She's Hazel's best friend, and we wanted to show our appreciation. As far as I'm concerned, you're a hero."

Because I was watching him so intently for his reaction, I saw his subtle flinch, but he covered it immediately by stiffening his shoulders and pasting a polite smile on his face. "Thank you, but all I did was call 911. Anybody else could have done the same."

"But you're the one who acted so quickly while everyone else was panicking," she replied.

"Yes, give yourself some credit," my dad agreed.

Devon ducked his head and mumbled, "Thanks."

"Also, happy birthday," Mom added. "Hazel told me it was yesterday."

He looked sideways at me, since I was seated right next to him. Then he faced Mom and replied, "Thank you."

"You have the same birthday as Hazel," my dad remarked in surprise. "Isn't that something? The other two babies in the hospital nursery must have been you and your brother." He trailed off, obviously remembering that Devon's brother was dead. "Uh, anyway, you were born on the same day, and now you're friends."

Luckily, after that painful awkwardness, Mom distracted Devon by serving him a piece of cake. I contemplated bitterly that we weren't even friends, and that drove me to devour my own piece of cake for the comfort of its sweet, sugary goodness. When I had scraped the last bit of frosting off my plate, I glanced over and saw Devon watching me with an amused expression.

"What?" I demanded, suddenly feeling self-conscious despite my confrontational attitude.

He smiled, and I never wanted him to stop. "I haven't seen anyone enjoy cake that much since I was a kid."

Still mesmerized by the first real smile I had ever seen from him, I answered in a daze, "I like it so much."

He smirked, like he knew I wasn't talking about the cake, and my face heated with what I could imagine was one hell of a blush.

When my father cleared his throat, I was so embarrassed that I wanted to die. "So, Devon," he began.

Mom quickly cut him off, saving me from some mortifying version of the *what-are-your-intentions-toward-my-daughter* question that my dad was about to ask. "Would you like me to pack you a couple of slices to take home?" she asked.

"No thank you," he replied. "But it was delicious, and so kind of you." For a moment, there was strong emotion in his eyes, like he was affected by my mom's kindness. Then his polite mask slipped back into place, and he backed up from the table. "Thanks again for having me over."

"It was our pleasure," Mom said. "Come back again soon."

He gave her a brief smile and nodded toward my dad in parting. "Sir."

My father nodded back but didn't say anything.

I stood to walk Devon out, and I followed him to his truck. He had gone back to ignoring me, and was apparently prepared to leave without even a word to me. I fumed as I watched him get into the driver's seat, and my temper boiled over when he reached out to close the door.

Springing into the space to prevent him from shutting it, I glared up at him. "What the hell was that? Why'd you come over if you were just going to ignore me?"

"Gee, I don't know," he answered sarcastically. "Maybe because your parents were there."

His reply confused me. "I told you that they were going to be here. Well, I told you that my mom was going to be here," I amended. "Remember? I said she wanted to meet you."

"I thought you were joking," he retorted with an angry expression. "I didn't know you were going to invite me over for one thing and then ambush me with your parents instead. No girl has ever pulled that one on me before. What, exactly, were you trying to accomplish? Did you really think we'd get engaged if I met your parents? You must be crazy."

"Engaged!" I exclaimed. "We're not even dating."

"Well, at least you realize that," he remarked dryly. "I was really starting to wonder about your sanity."

"Wait," I said as I processed everything he'd said. "What did you think I invited you over for?" Even as I asked it, the answer came to me. He thought my parents weren't going to be home...

His flat look confirmed it, and my face burned at the mere thought of it. "But we haven't even kissed yet!" I blurted. It was the 'yet' that mortified me.

I was no longer able to hold his gaze, and I shuffled out of the way so he could close his truck door.

He didn't, and I was about to turn and flee back into my house when his astonished voice stopped me. "You're a virgin?"

If I thought I was blushing before, my face was on fire now. "You don't know that," I mumbled down to the driveway.

"You didn't give it up to the jock?" he pressed.

That had me glancing up sharply at him. "His name was Matt," I said, a flash of pain stabbing my heart as I spoke his name. "And we were only dating for a few months."

Too late, I realized that I had just confirmed his suspicion about my virgin status. "It's none of your business anyway," I flung at him belatedly.

"So, your criteria for sex is time," he said. "How long? How many months do you need?"

"As many as it takes to fall in love," I answered without thinking.

He pounced on that. "So, you weren't in love with him."

It was a statement, not a question, but I replied anyway. "I didn't get the chance," I told him sadly.

I saw the emotion in his eyes, but he quickly wrangled it under control. "Right. Well...bye."

Just as he reached for the door, I urgently stepped into the space again to prevent him from closing it. "His death wasn't your fault."

I had told him that before, but I realized now that he had changed the subject by telling me about my surprise party. He never acknowledged what I said, and I was desperate for him to hear me this time. "It wasn't your fault," I repeated, staring intently into his eyes. "There was no way you could have known. You didn't touch him, so you didn't know he was in danger."

For a moment, I thought that I was getting through to him. I could see him processing what I was saying and absorbing it. His gaze was softer and more accepting than I had ever seen it, and I felt more connected to him than I ever had before. Then he went distant before pain filled his eyes. He looked haunted and destroyed, and I sensed that the hurt ran much deeper than I could even imagine.

My heart broke for him. "Devon," I said and reached up to place my hand on his arm.

A jolt of electric awareness shot through me and set my pulse racing. I pulled my hand back in surprise and threw an astonished look at him.

His equally startled stare surprised me, because it meant he felt it too. His gaze slowly heated, melting my insides as it did.

"We have chemistry," he said, his voice low and sexy. "We'd be so hot together."

His scorching look incinerated me, proving his point. "Think about it, Hazel," he said seductively.

I was so under his spell that all he had to do was gesture with his hand for me to back up, and I was maneuvering myself out of the way so he could shut the truck door. His dark eyes lingered on me before he reversed out of my driveway and drove away.

Even after he was gone, it took me several moments to emerge from his bewitching power. I blinked back to myself in a disoriented state of bewilderment.

What had just happened? I felt like I needed to cool down yet blow off steam at the same time.

CHAPTER 6

went to visit Abby and told her everything that had happened with Devon at my house. Amazingly, she was already home, having been discharged from the hospital that morning. We talked alone in her room, so I was able to tell her about Devon wanting to have sex with me.

She stared at me in wide-eyed wonder. "Are you going to do it?"

"Of course not!" I exclaimed, surprised that she would even ask. "We're not even dating. All he wants is a hookup."

"Yeah," she said with a sigh of disappointment. "Too bad he didn't kiss you before asking you for sex. At least you would have gotten the kiss of your dreams."

I giggled at how she phrased that. "Of my dreams? I'm glad you didn't exaggerate it."

Yet I was wishing I had gotten a kiss from him. What would it have been like? My crush on him had been unrequited for so long that I'd only had vague daydreams about kissing him. But our chemistry was more intense than I had ever imagined.

"Think about it," Abby said. "With how much you like him, it would have to be the best kiss ever."

With a heavy sigh, I said, "Well, I'll never know, so..."

"Why not?" she asked. "Now that you know he likes you, you can just kiss him."

"What? No, I can't! Are you crazy? And why would you think he likes me?"

"Uh, because he wants to have sex with you. That kind of gave it away," she commented dryly.

"He's had sex with other girls, and he's not with them now," I pointed out. "It doesn't mean that he liked them. He just hooked up with them."

"Well, then he won't mind if you just kiss him," she reasoned.

I waved that off, knowing that I'd never have the courage to be so daring. "Anyway, how are you doing? I'm sorry I've been talking about me when you just came home from the hospital."

"No, I'm glad to be talking about something else besides my medical stuff," she declared. "It's a lot more fun to hear about you and Devon."

I opened my mouth to protest, and she lifted her hand to halt me. "I'm okay. I've got my medicine and an appointment with a specialist. They've got it under control. So, please, let's forget about all that for now. I'm tired of thinking about it."

"Okay," I agreed, hoping that everything really was okay. "So, speaking about guys, how do you feel about Kyle?"

She gaped at me. "Something happened with Kyle too?"

I shook my head. "Not with me and him. But, Abby, he likes you."

"No, he doesn't," she began in denial.

"He does," I interjected. "He admitted it."

"He did?" she asked in surprise.

"Yeah," I confirmed. "He was really upset when we didn't know if you'd be okay."

"That's because we're friends. He would have been just as worried about—"

"No," I interrupted. "He told me that now he knows how I felt when Matt..."

I trailed off without saying the word. "Anyway, that means he thinks of you in a romantic way."

I left out the part where he had actually admitted to me that he was in love with her. That was something a girl needed to hear directly from the guy, and I didn't want to take that moment away from her—or him. It was enough to let her know that he liked her, so that she would be prepared when she saw him.

I watched her process what I had told her, trying to gage her reaction. Impatient to know, I asked, "So, do you like him?"

She seemed to be lost in thought as she said, "I don't know. I always thought he liked you, so I never looked at him that way. I mean, he's cute, and I always wondered why you didn't like him back."

I pounced on that. "You think he's cute! That's a good start."

She looked at me with an unsure expression. "I don't know what to do. What should I say to him?"

I shrugged. "Wait and see what he says, I guess. Then go with what you feel. Give him a chance if you want to. Or not, if you don't."

She gave me a deadpan look. "You're a lot of help."

I lifted my shoulders in a helpless shrug. "You know I thought he was annoying. But he was different when they took you to the hospital. I've never seen him so serious and upset. He really cares about you, and that's the number one thing you want in a boyfriend. But attraction is important too, and I don't know if you feel that for him."

The light blush that brought color to her cheeks gave me the answer to that. "Oh," I exclaimed in surprise. "Why didn't you tell me?"

She looked away as she played with the hem of her t-shirt. "Like you said, you thought he was annoying. And I thought he liked you."

I felt bad that she hadn't been able to confide in me. But I had done the same thing by keeping my crush on Devon a secret from her too. I thought about how I had almost lost her. "Let's tell each other everything from now on. You can tell me anything. I'm your best friend!"

Her gaze swung back to me after my heartfelt declaration. "Yes," she agreed. "No more secrets."

That was why I immediately called her after my text conversation with Devon later that evening. I received a text from an unknown number that read: *This is Devon. I forgot to tell you that I'll pick you up tomorrow at 11:00.*

My pulse raced as I remembered his parting words to me earlier that day. *For what?*

Horseback riding. Unless you've changed your mind about the other thing

Hot embarrassment scorched my face, even though I was alone in my room. Why had I been so obvious about where my thoughts had gone? I should have asked him where we were going or even a simple one word why instead of for what.

I haven't.

Okay. A horseback ride for you

He texted nothing else, and I was too embarrassed to ask any more questions. Like how he had gotten my number. He also assumed that I would go. I could text him that I wasn't going, but the lure of getting to be with him while also getting to fulfill my childhood dream was too tempting to resist.

Abby also encouraged me to take this opportunity to kiss him. "Think of how romantic it will be," she gushed over the phone.

I sighed but didn't bother to argue with her that this wasn't a date. Devon was just fulfilling his promise to take me riding. He had said that he would, and he was apparently keeping his word regardless of the drama that had happened between us. That made me think that he was a nice guy.

But that night, I had a disturbing dream. I was standing on the street, and I saw a figure walking toward me. My heart began to pound in fear, and I wanted to run away. I was unable to move though, and that increased my terror. As the person got closer and came clearly into view, I could see that it was Devon. That should have calmed me, but it didn't. Because something wasn't right about him.

He was walking, for one thing, but that wasn't it. He looked the same otherwise, and my gaze searched his beautiful face for the source of my unease. When he smiled, I got my answer. It was a sinister smile that made my skin crawl.

"You're mine now," he said.

I awoke with a scream trapped in my throat. I was paralyzed in fear, and it took a moment for me to realize that I could move now. Relief flooded through me as I sat up in bed and swung my legs over the side to stand up.

It was just a dream. But what a bizarre dream it had been. I wondered why my mind had imagined Devon that way. Yes, he was often cold and unfriendly, but I had never felt threatened by him. He had never been scary.

And why couldn't I have had a good dream about kissing him? If it couldn't happen in real life, I should at least get to experience it in my dreams. What he said should have been sexy, but it had been terrifying.

I shuddered at the memory and tried to banish it from my thoughts. It didn't fade from my mind like most dreams did, and I was no longer keen on seeing Devon that day. As I got ready, I told myself not to be ridiculous. It hadn't been real, and I didn't have premonitions like my great-grandmother. Still, I half-expected him to step out of his truck and walk up to my door when he arrived.

My relief at seeing him approach my house in his wheelchair was a little weird. Of course, I'd want him to regain the ability to walk if he could. It was just my creepy dream that made that seem like a bad thing. I needed to forget about it and enjoy this gift Devon was giving me.

I ran out to greet him so he wouldn't have to climb the porch steps. "Hi! How are you? It's so nice of you to do this for me! Thanks so much!"

His dark eyes narrowed on me before he regarded me with a flat expression. "You don't have to be nervous. I'm not going to try anything. Yesterday was a misunderstanding, and it won't happen again."

"Oh, no, it's not that. It was this crazy dream I had," I blurted and waved it off dismissively.

His mouth curved into a sexy smirk. "About me?"

My face heated, and his smile turned wicked. "Not that kind of dream!"

"Uh huh," he said, clearly not believing me.

"It wasn't! It was like this scary version of you walking toward me." I gave him an apologetic look. "That sounds awful for me to say that, but it wasn't the walking part that scared me. It was your creepy smile." I shuddered again at the memory of it.

Devon's reaction chilled me even more. All the blood drained from his face as he stared at me. "You saw him?" he asked in a shocked voice.

"Um, yeah," I answered in confusion. "It was a weird dream."

His gaze sharpened on me. "What did he do to you?"

I found it strange how he kept referring to my dream Devon in the third person. "Nothing," I hastened to tell him so he wouldn't get the wrong idea again. "You didn't do anything. You just walked up to me with a creepy smile on your face."

His gaze searched mine, apparently looking to see if I was telling him the truth. "Did he say anything to you?"

I looked away from him. "No."

He immediately knew I was lying. "Hazel, what did he say to you?" he demanded.

"It doesn't matter. It was just a dream."

"Tell me," he insisted.

I looked at him. "Okay, but it's not how it sounds. He...you, didn't say it that way."

"Okay," Devon said.

My gaze shifted away from him again. "You're mine." I cringed after saying it. "Like I said, it didn't sound romantic or anything."

His silence drew my eyes to him in my need to know his reaction. His alarmed expression was a blow to my ego. "I'm not trying to hint at anything. It was just a stupid dream."

Comprehension slowly replaced the fear in his eyes. "I know. I wasn't thinking anything like that."

My embarrassment was cut short when he reached out to take my hand. The fluttering in my stomach wouldn't be quelled, although I knew what he was doing. He concentrated for a moment before pinning me with an intense look. "Tell me if you see him again."

I stared at him in bewilderment.

His grip on my hand tightened. "I mean it, Hazel. It's important. Promise that you'll tell me immediately."

"Okay," I agreed. "I promise."

Seemingly satisfied, he let go of my hand. "Let's go."

He spun himself around and glided toward his truck. I followed him in a confused daze and climbed up into the passenger seat. My mind was trying to make sense of our bizarre conversation. Why was it so important to him for me to tell him if I had another dream about him?

He seemed to relax, but our conversation was over until we arrived at his house. I stared at it, hardly able to believe that was where he lived. I knew he was rich, but I hadn't expected his home to be such a huge mansion. I was also surprised by how modern and brand new it looked.

"My father tore down the original house and had this monstrosity built," Devon said.

"But it's so pretty," I exclaimed, because it was. It had white stone walls and a dark blue roof. There was nothing ugly about it.

"The old place had history and character. It was in the family for generations. But my father doesn't appreciate anything like that. He demolished it as soon as he inherited it. He always wants something bigger and better. And it has to look perfect."

I wasn't sure how to respond to that, but I wanted to keep the conversation going. "Was it like Ropes Mansion?" I asked, referencing one of our most famous historic houses.

"It wasn't quite that old. Ours was built in 1900. But, yes, it was a similar size. Have you ever been inside Ropes Mansion?"

"No," I answered sheepishly. "I've seen it in Hocus Pocus, but I never bothered to actually take the tour. Have you gone inside it?"

"No. I was too young to care about it before the accident. And afterwards..."

He trailed off, and I thought he wasn't going to continue until he said, "Well, I had much more important things to do."

His caustic tone made me wonder if he meant the things he'd done weren't important, or if he actually didn't have much to do. Either way, his demeanor didn't invite questions about it.

The driveway was long and continued past the house. Devon drove all the way back, and we got out of the truck. I admired the stables, which matched the look of the mansion to a degree. They also had a dark blue roof and white walls.

Once inside, I marveled at the luxury. This was no simple barn. I stood on a gorgeous stone floor beneath a soaring dark wood ceiling embedded with lights that shone like stars. There was even a chandelier hanging from it! The large horse pens had the same richly textured dark wood on the bottom and black metal railing on the top.

Devon led me to a stall containing a magnificent black horse. "This is Midnight. He's mine."

I stood looking at him in awe. "He's beautiful."

"Don't try to touch him just yet. He'll get used to seeing you around." He led me to a smaller horse. "This is Sugar. She was my mom's horse."

I admired the pretty brown mare before I turned to look at Devon. "I'm sorry about your mom and your brother."

"It was a long time ago," he said, but I could see the flash of pain in his eyes.

He looked away from me and put his hand out for Sugar to nuzzle. "You try it. She's gentle and friendly."

For the first time since before Matt died, I experienced delight as the horse took to me. She nuzzled my hand, and I petted her silky coat. Wanting to share my happiness, I looked over at Devon and beamed at him.

"I've missed your smile," he said.

I didn't know how to respond to that. "Thank you for bringing me here."

I had never seen his brown eyes look so warm. "It made you feel better, didn't it? I know being around the horses always helps me."

"Yeah, it did. It's the best present I could have gotten," I said sincerely.

He actually smiled. "You haven't even ridden Sugar yet."

"But," I began uncertainly.

"It's okay," he interjected as if reading my mind. "My mom wouldn't have wanted her never to be ridden again. My cousin rides her regularly."

A man approached, and Devon introduced us. "This is George. He'll get Sugar ready for you. George, this is Hazel."

"Nice to meet you, Miss," he said and proceeded to go into the stall and put a saddle on Sugar.

Devon began to give me tips on how to mount the horse. Nervousness overrode my excitement. I hadn't been scared when I was a kid, but I hadn't known then everything that could go wrong. What if I fell off? What if I embarrassed myself in front of Devon? Not to mention that this was his deceased mother's horse. What if I did something wrong and it hurt its leg?

"It's okay," he said, probably seeing the panic on my face. "She won't hurt you."

"Ready, Miss?" George asked.

I couldn't back out now. Devon had gone through the trouble to arrange this for me, and George had already saddled up the horse. "Yes," I said and approached the stall while repeating Devon's instructions in my head.

Last time, my dad had just lifted me onto the pony at the fair. I had thought that I'd have to climb up from the ground this time, but I was happy to see that George had put out a three-step thing to get me up to the horse. He called it a block. That made it much easier for me to get up into the saddle while he made sure that Sugar stayed in place.

It was a little scary being up high on top of her, but her calm acceptance of me eased my fears that she would take off and throw me off. George held on to the reins and led her out of the stall at a leisurely walk. Devon trailed behind us and gave me tips about riding, his voice carrying over the sound of the horse's hooves on the stone floor.

George led Sugar into a huge riding arena, but Devon stopped at the entrance. I realized why when I looked at the ground and saw that it was covered with what looked like sand. He probably couldn't maneuver his wheelchair through it.

My attention shifted to George when he handed me the reins and told me how to control Sugar. With his instruction, we continued the same leisurely walk around the arena. We weren't going any faster, but my heart soared with exhilaration. I was doing it! I was riding a horse on my own. I started to feel more comfortable and secure in the saddle, and more attuned to the horse as we went around the long arena at least a dozen times.

George approached us and instructed me on how to bring Sugar to a halt. She responded to my cues, and I felt like I knew what I was doing, even though my success was probably due to how well-trained she was.

George took the reins and started leading her back to the hallway, where Devon waited for us. I smiled big at him, with all the exhilaration and happiness I was feeling. He had a smile for me too, one that was soft and pleased that I'd enjoyed his gift to me.

"Thank you so much! This was the best present ever!"

"You're welcome," he said. "Next time you can try a trot, now that you've gotten comfortable with riding."

"I get to come back again?" I exclaimed like a little kid who'd just been told that Santa was making a return trip to my house this year.

Devon laughed, actually laughed, and it was a rich, wonderful sound that delighted me as much as his unguarded, amused expression.

A warm atmosphere was between us as we made our way back

to Sugar's stall. I petted her silky neck before dismounting her by using the block again.

"I should get you home," Devon said. He glided over to Midnight and reached up to pet him. "Once he gets used to you, he'll let you touch him."

That meant that he was planning to have me come over again, and happiness surged through me at the thought that he liked having me here, and that I would get to do more riding. But as I watched him with Midnight, it hit me that he couldn't ride his own horse. He couldn't enjoy the very experience that he had given me. My heart broke for him in that moment.

"Don't you dare feel sorry for me."

A cold glare followed his angry words before he spun around and raced away toward the exit. I hurried after him, only realizing after I was outside that I'd forgotten to say goodbye to George. I didn't risk going back, because I didn't want to upset Devon any more than I already had.

I wasn't sure what to say to him. Denying that I had been feeling sorry for him would be an obvious lie. And why would that make him mad anyway? It meant that I empathized with him.

I tried to explain myself, in case he didn't understand that. "It's just that I liked riding so much, and I knew that you probably did too. But since...but now..."

I trailed off awkwardly, knowing even before he stopped and turned to pin me with his icy stare that I shouldn't have said anything at all.

"But now I can't ride, and I can't walk. Do you have any more obvious things to point out?"

"I'm sorry," I began, but he cut me off.

"Forget it. Let's just go." He spun away from me and continued to his truck.

I went to the passenger side and got in, keeping quiet in the tense atmosphere between us as he drove me home. It had been such a great day, but I'd ruined it by upsetting him. Why did I open my mouth about him not being able to ride his horse? But then I realized that I hadn't said anything about it at first. He was the one who started it by getting mad about the expression of sympathy on my face. And that was stupid.

I decided that if he wasn't going to have anything more to do with me anyway, then I didn't need to hold back my opinions. "You're being stupid."

"Please, stop with the compliments. You're making me blush. First, I'm physically inferior, and now mentally. A guy can only take so much praise before his ego gets out of control."

My mouth dropped open. "What are you talking about? I never said anything about you being inferior. I'm saying you're being stupid for getting mad at me because I have sympathy for you. It means that I care about you."

"It means that you pity me," he countered. "And that means you think I'm pathetic."

"What?" I exclaimed. "No, it doesn't!"

"Forget it. I don't want to argue about it."

But I did. I couldn't have him thinking that. "Devon, caring about someone means having empathy for them. It has nothing to do with—"

"Hazel!" he thundered so loud that it startled me. "Drop it! I don't want to hear it."

I shut my mouth and glared at him, but he didn't look at me. I shifted my gaze forward to stare out the windshield, like he was doing. Both of us stewed in silence until we arrived at my house.

"Thank you for letting me ride Sugar," I told him curtly.

He nodded and said, "Remember to tell me if you see him again."

"Who?" I asked in confusion.

He turned his head to look at me full on then, and something about the intensity in his eyes made a chill run down my spine. "The other me from your dream. Tell me right away if you see him."

"It was just a dream," I said, more confused than ever.

"I need to know," he insisted. "It's important. Don't ask me to explain why. Just promise you'll tell me."

"Okay," I agreed to humor him.

"Promise me," he demanded.

Still baffled by his preoccupation with this, I said, "I promise, Devon."

At least we weren't ending off on a sour note—or so I thought.

Having gotten the promise he wanted out of me, he turned his head to face forward again. "Forgive me for not walking you to your door."

I saw a bitter smirk on his lips as I realized that he was dismissing me with those words. I got out of his truck, and he started backing out of my driveway as soon as I was clear of his vehicle. He drove away without giving me another look, and anger sparked within me again until I replayed his words in my mind. He'd apologized for not *walking* me to my door.

He was so confident and self-assured that I had never imagined that bothered him. I recalled his comment about being inferior, and I felt heartsick for him. How could he think that? There was nothing inferior about him. Why was he suddenly thinking that there was?

Was it my fault? Had I made him feel that way by feeling bad for him for not being able to ride his horse? While it was sad, that didn't seem like a big enough reason for him to feel inferior. It wasn't like I was a champion rider.

Could it have been because I hadn't wanted to sleep with him? That couldn't be it either, since he'd had sex with other girls —girls who were much more popular than I was. And he'd been the one to withdraw from the popular crowd, not the other way around.

What was it then? I had to have done something to bring this on all of a sudden. I thought over our interactions today and landed on his weirdness about my dream. As it hit me, I felt like an idiot for not realizing it sooner. I'd told him about a walking version of himself. It must have been festering in his mind the whole time we were together.

Did he perceive it as some kind of criticism about his inability to walk? I'd told him that the walking version of him in my dream had been scary, but he must not have focused on that part. And he wanted me to tell him if I dreamt about him again.

There was no way I was ever going to mention it to him again. I hoped I never had another creepy dream like that again. But if I did, he wasn't going to know about it.

CHAPTER 7

Unfortunately, I had a disturbing dream about creepy Devon that very night. He rode a black horse that looked like a demon version of Midnight. It had glowing red eyes and sharp, pointed teeth when it opened its mouth to bare them at me. I stumbled back in terror.

Creepy Devon reigned him in and directed a mocking smile at me. "Don't worry. He knows who his master is. I can control my stallion. Unlike that pathetic weakling who can't even ride his horse. Why he clings to that existence is beyond me."

Anger overrode my fear. "He is not pathetic or weak! He's amazingly strong and good. Who cares if he can't ride a horse? He's smart and beautiful and—"

"I'm more beautiful," he declared, cutting me off. "You can have the better, complete man."

He dismounted from the beast and reached out to me. "Just take my hand."

He was so handsome, with all of Devon's dark good looks. He was right about not having any physical imperfections. Yet he was wrong about being more beautiful than Devon. He was lacking that inner fire and complexity that the real Devon had—the very essence of him. He was perfect on the outside, but empty and soulless on the inside.

I had no desire to take his hand, and I instinctively knew that it would be bad if I did. "No," I stated firmly. "Leave me alone."

He sneered at me, revealing some of the ugliness hidden beneath that gorgeous exterior. "I'll remember you said that when you're begging me for my help. You had the chance to do this the easy way, but you think you're better than me. I offered you everything, but now you'll get scraps."

I scoffed at that. "I don't want anything from you. Go back to where you came from."

He seemed to be obeying me as he returned to his demon horse and mounted it. But once astride it, he smiled that creepy smile he'd had in my first dream about him. "You'll join me there soon. Then we'll see if you still want nothing from me."

I awoke with those ominous words striking fear in my heart. Telling myself it was just a dream didn't comfort me. My primal instincts were warning me not to ignore the threat. Yet that was ridiculous. A dream posed no danger to me, because none of it was real.

What also disturbed me about it were the things creepy Devon had said about the real Devon. I certainly didn't think that way about him, so why had I imagined such cruel criticisms of him? I ended up chalking it up to Devon's false belief in his inferiority. It had spilled over into my dream, and I had essentially argued with his fantasy walking version of himself about it.

I wished that I could tell him how I had rejected that version of him, but I didn't want to trigger him again. It was best not to mention it at all.

So, I went to school and immersed myself in my normal life. I took in all the sensory details, from the sound of clanging locker doors and chatter of students in the hallways, to the smell of chalk in the classroom, to the vibrant red lipstick a girl in one of my classes was wearing. This was real—not the creepy guy on a demon horse. He was only a figment of my imagination.

Yet most people would say that seeing a ghost wasn't real either, but there was no other way to explain how I would have known where to find Svetlana's body. But I had seen her while I was awake, so that also made it obvious that sinister Devon wasn't real. Not unless he was an actual demon haunting my dreams.

That was a horrifying thought that sent a shiver of dread down my spine. As much as I wanted to dismiss it as a ridiculous idea, I couldn't. If ghosts were real, then other supernatural things could be real too. I wished that I could talk to my great-grandmother. If it was true that she could see the future, she would have been able to warn me if I was in danger. For a moment, I considered trying to contact her through a Ouija board. But what if the demon came through instead? Opening myself up to the supernatural probably wasn't the best idea.

Then I remembered that I knew someone who could sense danger. All I had to do was get him to touch me. I looked across the cafeteria to where he sat alone at his table. He still exuded such an unapproachable presence, but I knew that he wasn't as cold and forbidding as he looked.

He'd allowed me to get a glimpse into his life, and I didn't want him to shut me out again. I knew now that my crush on him was hopeless. He didn't want a relationship, and I didn't want a hookup. But that didn't mean that we couldn't be friends.

He didn't seem lonely, but who didn't need a friend? It wasn't good for him to be alone all the time. I didn't know why he had ditched his popular friends. Maybe because a crowd was too much? It made sense then for him to have one really good friend, and that person could be me. He had to at least find me tolerable if he had invited me over to ride his mom's horse. That had to be something special that he didn't let just anyone do. And he had come to my birthday party. Which was also his birthday. That at least told me that he hadn't wanted to be alone on his birthday—whether he admitted it or not.

And he would never admit it, I realized. He was the kind of person who would die of loneliness before ever admitting that he needed someone. Was it pride or stubbornness?

Either way, I made my decision to try to be his friend. I stood up and lifted my tray with my half-eaten lunch. "I'll see you guys later."

"Where are you going?" Sarah asked.

"To talk to a friend," I answered but didn't linger to explain.

Abby was the only one of my friends I'd told about going horseback riding at Devon's place. She wasn't back at school yet, and I wasn't going to talk about Devon at school anyway. I hoped that Sarah picked up on me calling him a friend when she saw who I was on my way to talk to.

It was reminiscent of my walk to his table a couple of years ago, especially when he noticed me approaching and locked eyes with me. He still sat at the same table on the outer edge of the cafeteria, so there was no doubt that I was headed there. He didn't look away and dismiss me this time, but he wasn't exactly welcoming.

"What are you doing?" he demanded as I set my tray down and took the seat across from him.

"I'm having lunch with you," I replied and picked up my chicken sandwich to take another bite.

He scowled at me. "Did I ask you to sit here?"

I shrugged. "No."

Of course, I would leave if he told me to. I wasn't a stalker who would force my presence on him. In the meantime, I took another unconcerned bite of my sandwich. I had done the hard part by risking rejection. It was completely up to him what happened next. That took all the pressure off of me.

I could feel him staring at me, but I looked at my food and the hallway past the exit. Anywhere but at him, because I didn't want this to come off as a confrontation.

After a moment, he said, "Whatever. Do what you want."

I kept my victory smile on the inside, not letting it show on my face. I knew that would be a mistake with him. I had to act cool, and like this wasn't a big deal. Instinct told me that he wouldn't be open to declarations of friendship. I had to go slow and make this all seem normal.

But he threw me off immediately with a question I should have anticipated. "Did you see him again?"

I had just taken a drink from my water bottle, and I swallowed it the wrong way, erupting into a coughing fit.

"I'll take that as a yes," he said dryly.

"It went down the wrong way," I said between coughs, hoping that if I didn't respond to his statement, he'd let it drop. I didn't want to outright lie to him, because I wanted to gain his trust. It was the only way to form a real friendship with him.

He leaned forward and pinned me with his piercing dark gaze. "You promised to tell me, Hazel."

I slumped in defeat. "I did." With a sigh, I admitted, "I had another dream."

"What did he do to you?" he demanded.

"Nothing!" I exclaimed, disturbed that he thought something that happened in a dream mattered. My theory about it being a demon grew into a suspicion. "Do you know something about this? Have you seen him too?"

His gaze shifted away from me, and I jumped on his unconscious tell. "You have! That's why you're so obsessed with me seeing him, because you know he's real." I shivered at the creepy realization and caught his eyes with mine. "Is he a demon pretending to be you? I've heard that they can take the forms of people you know to trick you."

"He can't hurt you if you don't summon him."

His calm words sent a chill down my spine. If he had meant them to be soothing, he had failed. He'd just confirmed that an evil entity was haunting my dreams, and that it wanted to hurt me.

Devon stared at me with all his intimidating intensity. "What I want to know is how you contacted him in the first place. Were you playing with a Ouija board?"

"I knew that would be a bad idea!" I declared triumphantly. "That's why I decided not to try to get answers about him that way."

"But that's how you first contacted him?" he asked.

I shook my head. "No. I don't know why I suddenly started dreaming about him."

"What about doing spells?" he questioned. "Have you been messing around with anything like that?"

"What?" I asked, truly bewildered. "You know that witches aren't real, right? All that witchcraft stuff is fun for tourists, but it's all fake."

The silent pause before he responded made me wonder if he actually did believe in witchcraft. Despite having the impression that he could be a warlock in a fantasy world, his belief in such a thing didn't fit with his personality at all.

"Right," he said. "I was just checking if you were into anything like that." He turned his attention to his lunch and cut into his partially eaten chicken breast, spearing a piece with his fork and lifting it to his mouth.

That's when I noticed that he was using real utensils instead of the plastic ones provided by the cafeteria. He'd obviously brought his lunch from home, and it wasn't a sandwich like most people packed. It was a homemade meal with a side of vegetables, and it was in what appeared to be a stainless-steel container.

"Are you eating that cold?" I asked. "You can't put metal in the microwave." Not that we had access to a microwave, so I wasn't sure why I'd mentioned that.

"Yes," he said. "It's the healthiest way to eat it. Microwaving your food isn't good for you, and microwaving it in plastic is even worse. Keeping it in plastic at all is not good."

He glanced at my lunch. "It's terrible that they serve students processed food. You don't even have a vegetable on your plate."

I pointed at my fries. "Potatoes are a vegetable."

"The only healthy way to eat them is baked. Cooking them in oil destroys any health benefits they might have."

I rolled my eyes. "We don't have to worry about that kind of stuff yet. My mom says to enjoy it now, because I'll have to watch what I eat when I get to be her age."

"That's bad advice. Heart disease can start in your teens if you eat a lot of—"

My outburst came out of nowhere as I exclaimed, "Heart disease! It wasn't the food she ate that almost killed Abby. It's not what killed Matt, and it's not what killed Svetlana either. So, I'm not going to worry about eating French fries, because I'm going to enjoy my life while I can." I grabbed one and shoved it into my mouth for good measure, chewing it as I gave him a look of defiance.

He watched me without comment for a moment but then asked, "Who is Svetlana?"

I froze as I realized that I had blurted out her name to him. Swallowing down my salty French fry, I grabbed my bottle of water and took a sip. "Um, she was a little girl who drowned."

He eyed me suspiciously. "Why are you so nervous? Was it your fault that she drowned?"

My mouth dropped open in shock. "How could it be my fault? Why would you even think that?"

His stare was unwavering as he watched me like a hawk. "Maybe you weren't paying attention when you were babysitting her, and she fell in the pool. That happened to me when I was little. Luckily, my brother was there and ran to get our nanny. She got me out and manipulated us into not telling our parents."

"That's awful," I said, unsettled by the story, and by his negligent nanny. "I would never do that. I wasn't babysitting Svetlana. I knew her when I was a kid."

His expression softened with understanding. "She was one of your friends, and she died. That's a lot for a kid to deal with. How old were you when it happened?"

"Oh, I don't remember her," I explained. "So, I wasn't upset."

"You don't remember her, but you know what happened to her?" he questioned in confusion.

I waved that off. "My mom told me about her. Anyway, my point is that people die from other things besides heart disease, and eating what you want is okay as long as you eat healthy stuff too."

But he wouldn't let it go, and my attempt to steer him away from Svetlana failed. "Why would your mom tell you about it if you didn't remember it? Why would she bring it up at all? I'd think she'd be happy you didn't remember such a traumatic experience."

"We were talking about something else, and it came up. Anyway, it wasn't traumatic for me."

"It had to be," he argued. "That's probably why you've blocked it out. Having a friend die at that age must have been too much for your little kid brain to handle."

Frustration with his refusal to drop the subject and with how wrong he was about his assumptions had me blurting, "She was already dead when I met her."

That shut him up, and I had instant regret as he stared at me in silence. I dropped my eyes to my tray of food and went back to eating, seeking comfort in the familiar taste of my fries and chicken sandwich. Now Devon would think that I was crazy.

My mind scrambled for a way to fix this, but I could think of nothing to say. Claiming that I was joking would come off as tasteless and insensitive, because there was nothing funny about the death of a little girl.

"You see dead people?" he asked.

I cringed, even though he hadn't said it in a mocking way. Daring to lift my eyes to look at him, I saw him studying me with an unreadable expression. It wasn't exactly comforting, but at least it wasn't outright questioning my sanity.

"Only her," I told him. "And that's according to my mom. I don't remember any of it."

"Tell me," he demanded.

So, I did. When I was done, I awaited his judgement, like he was some sort of god.

To my surprise, he didn't declare me insane and order me to stay away from him. "That's why you can see him," he said as if speaking to himself. "Because of your psychic ability."

"No," I corrected him. "It was my great-grandma who was a psychic. It was just a one-time thing with me."

His gaze sharpened on me. "Your great-grandmother had psychic abilities? Tell me."

Again, I obeyed his demand and told him everything that my

mom had told me about her. He listened intently as he ate his chicken breast and vegetables. This time, I felt oddly comfortable sharing this weird story with him—maybe because it wasn't about me. After I finished, I resumed eating my lunch as I let him process what I'd just told him.

He didn't speak until he'd taken the last bite of his food and set down his fork. He drank from his metal bottle and then looked at me. "You have your great-grandmother's ability, but you haven't developed it. You've only tapped into it when the influence on you was strong, like with Svetlana wanting you to help find her body."

His expression turned grim. "And with him wanting you to see him."

I had a sudden thought and blurted it out unthinkingly. "Is it your twin? Is his ghost contacting me?"

"No!" he exclaimed vehemently.

I'd never seen him react so strongly to anything, and I stared at him, stunned into silence.

He leaned toward me and lowered the volume of his voice. "Brax was thirteen when he died, and he wasn't evil. This is... something else."

He'd just confirmed that this entity was evil, and a chill went through me. "A demon?" I asked fearfully.

His answer scared me even more. "I don't know. I don't know what I summoned."

My mouth dropped open in shock. I leaned in toward him and asked in quiet disbelief, "You summoned it?"

Our eyes held for a moment, and I saw the remorse in his before he pulled back and slipped behind his mask of indifference. "Yes, Hazel, I do black magic in my spare time. How gullible are you? I could probably tell you that I'm a leprechaun, and you'd believe it."

"Are you kidding?" I said, getting annoyed. "You think you can drop something like that on me and pretend it's a joke? Hell no! I want to know everything about it—right now."

He gazed at me with infuriating calmness. "There's nothing

to tell. I played along with your ridiculous claim about seeing dead people, but I don't believe any of it. Like you said, it's all for the tourists."

I almost called him out on his crap. He'd been the one to bring up a Ouija board and spells, and I had told him that witchcraft wasn't real. That had been before I had mentioned anything about Svetlana. But if I pointed all that out and argued with him, I would never get any answers from him. He would probably get mad and shut me out entirely. I didn't want to lose the progress I'd made by getting him to eat lunch with me. I had to stay on his good side so that I could get him to drop his guard with me.

I tried to mirror his unaffected attitude. "To be fair, my mom said that I saw a dead person. I don't remember it, so I can't say for sure if I did or didn't."

A gleam of amusement brightened his dark eyes as he watched me, and the butterflies in my stomach took notice. I wanted to see more of that brightness hidden within him. I knew it was there, just out of reach, if only I could find my way through the darkness keeping it contained.

The mirth faded from his gaze, but the light remained. "You look at me like you don't see it," he said in a tone of wonder.

"See what?" I asked, completely clueless about what he was talking about.

That brought forth a small laugh that made my breath catch in my throat. In our entire time in high school, I'd never seen or heard him laugh before, not even when he was part of the popular crowd. This realization pierced my heart, but I told myself that just because I hadn't seen it didn't mean it never happened. He wasn't in my sights all the time. He must have laughed sometimes. If not at school, then at home. But I remembered how he had spent his birthday with me, and I wondered again about his situation at home.

On instinct, I reached out to touch his hand. His eyes met mine and held. Magic flowed between us, igniting sparks of energy that rushed along my nerve endings down to my fingertips. It crackled into his hand and jumped back into mine, stronger from the contact with him. Power surged through me, and I craved closer contact with him, knowing that if we were joined, we'd be invincible.

He sucked in a sharp breath and let go of my hand, jolting me back to reality. The way he stared at me like I might attack him at any moment made it clear he hadn't had the same magical experience as I'd had when I touched his hand.

I'd touched him.

My eyes went wide with fear. "Did you see something bad? Am I going to die?"

"Of course not," he said, but he was no longer looking at me as he quickly gathered his things.

I stood up and grabbed my lunch tray to hurry after him. I was slowed down by having to dump my garbage in the trash, so he was already speeding down the hallway when I rushed out of the cafeteria. I sprinted to catch up to him, but he went into the boys' bathroom to evade me.

I halted and only debated for seconds before barging in after him. He turned at the sound of my footsteps and looked annoyed rather than surprised. "Are you lost?"

Fortunately, no one else was there. I glanced in distaste at the urinals. The entire idea of it seemed gross and embarrassing to me. But I had more important things on my mind. "What did you see?"

He expelled an exasperated breath. "Nothing. Now can I have some privacy?"

"Then why'd you leave the cafeteria so fast?" I demanded.

He glanced around before fixing a mocking gaze on me. "I don't know. Could it be that I had to go to the bathroom?"

Unconvinced, I crossed my arms and stared him down.

He stared right back at me with an obstinate expression. Then his mouth quirked into a smirk as my eyes went wide in panic at the sound of male voices in the hallway. I spun away from him and dashed out of the restroom just as two guys were about to enter.

"Sorry! Wrong one," I exclaimed, hoping they'd believe my lie about being in there by mistake.

I heard them laughing as I fled into the girls' restroom across the hall. I couldn't believe I'd done that, but it had been worth it. Devon's little smirk at the end had reassured me. He probably wouldn't have found anything funny about the situation if he'd had a premonition about my death. No matter how much he pretended not to care about anyone, he'd already proven that he did.

What bothered me now was what he'd said about summoning that entity that looked like him. I knew that hadn't been a joke. I'd seen the remorse in his eyes. He'd done something, and I needed to know what it was.

Maybe if I found out how he'd summoned it, I'd be able to figure out a way to get rid of it. I had to try, and I wasn't going to leave Devon alone until he told me.

CHAPTER 8

Devon was apparently just as determined to tell me nothing as I was to get the truth out of him. He tried ignoring me as I walked beside him in the parking lot after school.

When we got to his truck, he turned a cold stare on me. "Do you know what those guys thought we were doing in the bathroom? I told them you accidentally walked into the wrong one, and they said you told them the same story, but they didn't believe it. The rumors will only get worse if they see you chasing after me like a puppy."

My stomach sank at that news, and anger at him ignited into a rant. "That's your fault! I wouldn't have been in there if you had talked to me. Everything is your fault. Even this creepy demon coming after me in my dreams. You better tell me how you summoned it!"

His own anger sparked, burning away the ice in his gaze. "I didn't ask for you to come crashing into my life like a damn wrecking ball. This is why I don't get involved in anyone's crap. I don't need your crazy shit about demons and witchcraft."

"You're the one who brought up witchcraft, not me. That's it," I realized. "You did some kind of spell."

"Do you hear yourself?" he demanded. "That's crazy."

"That's what you tried to tell me about your psychic power," I reminded him. "This isn't any crazier than that. Tell me what you did."

We both fell silent as several students walked past us and cast speculative looks at us. I couldn't help flushing in embarrassment as I wondered if they'd heard the rumors Devon had told me about.

"Get in," he said curtly. "I'll give you a ride."

"I'll bet he will," one of the girls called out and giggled.

My face now in flames, I scurried to climb up into the passenger seat of his truck.

Devon got in the driver's side and slammed the door shut. "I warned you."

The rumors were mortifying, but I wasn't going to get sidetracked from my mission to learn the truth. "What kind of spell was it?"

"A love spell," he quipped. "Did it work?"

My stomach did a little flutter, even though I knew he didn't mean it. He didn't like me enough to ask me out on a date, let alone to cast a spell to gain my affections. "Be serious," I demanded. "I want to know how you summoned him."

He turned on his truck and backed out of his parking space. "I told you that was all a joke."

"No, it wasn't," I insisted. "Just tell me what you did, so I can figure out a way to get rid of him."

"How about stay away from me," he suggested as he followed the line of cars out of the parking lot. "He didn't bother you until you started talking to me. So, if you stop talking to me, he'll probably leave you alone."

That made sense, but it also felt wrong. I didn't want to let go of Devon now that he was finally part of my life, but it was more than that. Instinct told me that we were stronger together than apart.

"No, he won't," I said, feeling the truth of my words as I spoke them. "We need to fight him together."

He scoffed. "Fight him? How are you going to do that? He's not here, Hazel. You only see him when you're asleep, and he can't hurt you in your dreams."

"That's what they said about Freddy Kruger," I muttered.

Devon glanced at me sharply before returning his eyes to the road. "He can't hurt you. He would have already killed me if he could."

I looked at him in horror. I'd been exaggerating with my Freddy Kruger comment. "He kills people?"

He hesitated before answering, and that set off alarm bells in my mind. "No," he said. "I just told you that he can't."

His reply didn't reassure me. Can't didn't mean he wouldn't. What if he found a way? Whatever he was, he was a threat. I had to find a way to get rid of him. If Devon wouldn't help me, then I'd have to do it on my own.

But how? I didn't know anything about witchcraft. Where would I find the spell I needed? Where had Devon found whichever spell he had used?

"Don't break your brain," he said dryly.

I glanced at him. "What?"

He took one hand off the wheel and gestured toward me. "You looked like you were trying to solve the world's toughest math equation. What were you thinking about so hard over there?"

I went ahead and blurted it out. "Are you a warlock?"

He sputtered a laugh and gave me an amused look. "Nobody's ever asked me that before."

"I'm serious," I said in frustration. "How else would you know how to do spells?"

"And your mind went straight to warlock? Most people would assume that I'd found a witch to do the spell for me."

"I guess because you look like one. But you found a witch? I didn't think of that. I was trying to think of where to find a spell book, but that's a good idea. What's her name?"

He pulled into my driveway and turned to me with a bewildered expression. "You think I look like a warlock?"

"It's not a bad thing," I assured him. "They're strong and powerful." *And hot.*

He stared at me. "That's how you see me?" His quiet words contrasted the growing intensity of his gaze.

"Yes," I answered, my voice coming out soft and breathy.

Heat flared in his eyes, and he leaned in toward me.

I moved toward him too, drawn like a moth to the flame. Excited butterflies swooped in my belly, and my breath hitched in anticipation as the distance between our mouths disappeared. My eyes drifted closed, and I felt his lips brush over mine. The gentle touch of them sent an electric spark through me that awakened all my nerve endings.

I pressed my lips more firmly to his, wanting more of this irresistible contact. He groaned and deepened the kiss. His tongue caressed mine in a delicious dance that made me hungry for more. I couldn't get enough, and neither could he. We kissed until we had to stop to catch our breaths.

Breaking physical contact didn't break our connection. It was in the charged air between us—some kind of magical energy that pulsed with an exhilarating power. I could see that Devon felt it too.

Vitality and masculine power radiated from his gaze, and he once again reminded me of a warlock, imbued with supernatural secrets and knowledge. Something deep within me responded and unfurled, being drawn toward the surface.

Alarm suddenly flashed in his eyes, and his expression shut down like a curtain coming down to hide the stage. I could no longer see anything that he was feeling. "That was hot. But since it's all I'm going to get from you, there's no reason to do it again."

That stung, and I struggled to hide my hurt that he didn't want to kiss me again. I had daydreamed about it for so long, and it had finally happened and been just as magical as in my fantasies. I'd thought that it had been the same for him, but that had obviously been wishful thinking. Because he was rejecting me right after kissing me.

Fearing that my voice might give away how upset I was, I

directed what I hoped was a glare at him and got out of his truck, slamming the door and walking quickly in a semblance of storming off. Really, I was just rushing into the house before the tears brimming in my eyes could fall.

I was glad my parents weren't home yet from work to see me crying. I could let loose and sob my heart out. I'd always known that my crush on Devon was unrequited, but I'd still held out hope that maybe someday he might like me back. That hope was shattered now. If he had no feelings for me after kissing me, then he never would.

Being friends wasn't possible now either. That spectacular kissing session—and his rejection of me—would always stand between us. It hadn't been just one little kiss. We might have been able to get past the awkwardness of that and become friends. But there was no way we could ignore the electric, drugging kisses we had shared and pretend that we could have a platonic relationship.

So now, I could have nothing with him.

"Not necessarily," Abby said over the phone.

I'd called her after I was done crying and could speak well enough to tell her what had happened. I needed my best friend to commiserate with me and comfort me.

Instead, she was trying to give me false hope. "It's not like he didn't like kissing you. He said it was hot. The only thing stopping him from doing it again is the sex thing. But when he sees you're not falling for that, he'll want a real relationship with you. Just give him some time to realize how much he wants to be with you."

I knew that was wishful thinking, but it was hard not to hope that she was right. "Abby! You're supposed to be telling me what an asshole he is, and to forget him."

"I would if I thought I was wrong. But seeing you guys together at your birthday party...well, I've never seen that kind of chemistry in real life before. I could understand why you were still crushing on him while you were with Matt. He was a great boyfriend, but you guys didn't have those kinds of sparks."

Guilt sliced through me. Here I was crying over another guy

while my boyfriend was dead. It hadn't even been a full two months yet, and I'd already moved on. What a selfish, insensitive person I was.

I had to change the subject, so I blurted out, "I need a witch!"

There was a pause before Abby asked slowly, "To do a love spell?"

"No," I exclaimed with a sputtered laugh. Then I sobered, because this was serious. "I've been having these dreams."

I told her about them, and about how Devon had let it slip that he didn't know what he had summoned. "What if it's a demon? I have to find some way to get rid of it."

"That's so creepy!" Abby said. "I can't believe that this is your life."

"I know," I agreed. "I just want to go back to normal. If this thing could be summoned, there has to be some way to send it back to wherever it came from. That's why I need to find a witch."

"Well, that's what Salem is famous for. It'll be easy to find a witch here."

Except it wasn't. We found plenty of people claiming to be witches, but they were trying to sell us crystals and read our fortunes. A few seemed offended when I mentioned that I wanted to get rid of a demon. They gave me a lecture about messing with dark magic and said that they practiced good magic. Others offered me protection spells—for a price.

I decided I'd rather spend my money on a cappuccino I knew I liked rather than a protection spell I didn't know would work. Abby and I sat down in the coffee shop to take a break and enjoy our tasty beverages.

"Are you allowed to have that?" I asked belatedly, suddenly remembering her heart condition.

"Yes," she answered. "I don't have heart disease. It's a birth defect."

"How are you doing?" I asked, feeling like a bad friend for not putting that ahead of my demon problem.

"Fine," she said with a shrug. "It's not like I had any symptoms before I passed out at your party. I can't feel any difference now either. The only change is that I take medicine for it now."

A surge of gratefulness for Devon's actions that night had me softening toward him. He'd saved my best friend's life. So, he'd rejected me and broken my heart. What was that in comparison to having Abby here alive and well?

"Hey, I've got an idea. You can use your psychic power to find a witch," she suggested.

I gave her a bewildered look. "Did I miss part of the conversation? Weren't we just talking about your health?"

"Yeah, and that got me thinking about how Devon saved me and saved you with his psychic power. And that made me think about you and the ghost of that little girl, and your psychic power."

"That happened when I was a little kid. I don't even remember it! If I ever did have psychic powers, they're gone now. Otherwise, I would have been able to save Matt," I added bitterly.

"Hazel," she said gently and reached out to touch my hand. "You know that's not your fault. There's no way you could have known that would happen."

"Then why do you think I'll be able to find a witch with this power I don't have?" I challenged.

"Well, you might not," she admitted. "But it's worth a try, since we're out of options." She took both my hands in hers. "Okay, close your eyes and reach out with your mind."

"Abby, we're not doing a séance. Why are we holding hands?"

She shrugged without letting go of my hands. "I don't know, but that's how they do it in movies. Close your eyes and concentrate."

I glanced around the coffee shop to see if anyone was watching us. Right now, we could possibly pass for a same sex couple. But if I closed my eyes and sat there like I was in a trance, people would definitely notice the weirdness of us.

I made eye contact with a man and quickly looked away. "Maybe we should do this at my house," I suggested.

"But we're already here in town where she probably is. You might have more luck reaching her if you're closer to her."

"Abby, this is stupid," I complained.

She fixed a serious look on me. "Are you worried about what people will think, or are you worried about getting rid of this demon?"

She had a point. As unlikely as this was to work, I felt obligated to at least give it a shot. My only other choice was to pay for a protection spell that also might not work. At least this was free.

"Okay, I'll do it," I said, ignoring the embarrassment and committing to it.

I saw Abby's excited smile before I closed my eyes. She was probably expecting some thrilling supernatural thing to happen, but she was about to be disappointed. I tried to clear my mind of such thoughts and focus on finding a real witch.

Instead, my mind conjured up Devon's disapproving face. "Hazel! What the hell are you doing?" he demanded.

"Leave me alone," I answered him in my thoughts, even though I knew I was just imagining him talking to me. "You don't care about me, so just leave me alone."

"I do care," he protested, but I blocked him out.

Next, I was in the void, an empty place that was like a rest stop between destinations. I could go in any direction, and I took a moment to get my bearings and feel out where to go. There were so many possible threads I could follow, but I had to pick out the right one. Before I could, an angry voice intruded on my peaceful perusal of the possibilities.

"You think you can banish me?"

It was *him*. The demon.

He scoffed. "I'm not a demon. Is that why you're afraid of me? Foolish girl, there is no need to fear me. I'm a man, like that pathetic excuse for a man you're fixated on, except better."

"Stop saying that you're better than him! You're not," I insisted.

"I am. In fact, you could say that I'm his better half."

I gasped as the pieces fell into place. Why Devon would be

doing a spell to summon this entity. Why it looked exactly like him, except for the ability to walk. "Are you his twin?"

He laughed, sounding delighted that I'd guessed correctly. "Smart girl," he praised. "You've proven yet again why you're perfect for me."

I ignored that statement, wanting answers instead of to get into an argument. "So, you're a ghost?"

"I'm no more a ghost than he is," he said, sounding offended.

"Then how am I talking to you if you're dead?"

"Because I'm not," he replied like that made perfect sense.

I wondered if he somehow didn't know, and I gently told him, "I'm sorry, but you were killed in an accident when you were thirteen."

"Do I look thirteen?" he challenged.

That took me aback, although it was so obvious that I wondered how it hadn't occurred to me right away.

"If I was dead, wouldn't I have stopped aging?"

"But it was on the news. I looked up articles about it after I met Devon. And there was a funeral for you and..."

"Yes, my poor mother died," he said. "But I didn't. I was in a coma when I was taken to the hospital, and Devon convinced the doctor to pronounce me dead."

"What?" I exclaimed in disbelief. "Why would he do that?"

"She," he corrected me, misunderstanding who I was talking about. "The doctor was a she—our uncle's wife, in fact. And she did it because she was in love with Devon."

"He was thirteen!"

"Yes, sick, I know. She's much younger than our uncle, but was still an adult lusting after a child. Devon used it to his advantage and had her get me out of the way so he could inherit everything."

I couldn't believe any of this. "You're lying! He wouldn't do that."

"Wouldn't he? How well do you really know him? You think you're an expert on him because he showed you his horse and stuck his tongue in your mouth? He's done much more than that with other girls, but he never revealed his true self to them either."

"You could see us?" I asked, mortified that he had watched us kiss. I didn't even want to think about the possibility that he had seen Devon in much more intimate situations with other girls.

His expression suddenly changed, and he said in an urgent tone, "Help me, Hazel! He's got me trapped."

CHAPTER 9

n the next instant, I was yanked away from him by a hand on my arm. "Get away from him right now," a voice demanded.

It was a voice talking to me in person, not in my mind. And the hand really had a hold of my arm. I opened my eyes and blinked at the sight of Devon glaring at me. "What are you doing?"

"What am I doing? What the hell are *you* doing? You blocked me, but not him? Why would you connect to his mind like that? Don't you know that makes him stronger?"

"No," I shot back. "I didn't know any of that, because you wouldn't tell me anything."

"All you need to know is to stay away from him."

I yanked my arm out of his grasp. "Because you say so? I don't think so." I narrowed my eyes at him. "And why don't you want me to know about him? What are you hiding?"

"Nothing! What the hell is your problem? Why are you so obsessed with him all of a sudden? I thought you wanted to get rid of him, and now you're having seances to talk to him?"

I didn't want to believe the things his twin had said, but I couldn't help my growing suspicion. "Why don't you want me to talk to him?"

Instead of answering me, he went on the offensive. "What'd

he say to you to get you on his side? Did he promise to marry you when he gets my inheritance? Don't count on it. He's only out for himself."

My stomach dropped. Devon had just confirmed that we were talking about his twin. Who else would be able to get his inheritance? And he would surely get it after their father found out what Devon had done and disowned him. He would probably go to jail too.

"Hazel, what's wrong?" Abby asked, drawing my attention to her. "You look like you've seen a ghost." She glanced around warily. "Is it still here?"

"He's no ghost," Devon said bitterly, plunging another knife in my heart.

I stared at him, aghast and still hardly believing it. "How could you do that to him? And to your dad."

His jaded smile held no warmth. "So, you agree that he deserves a son who isn't defective. Well, I'm sorry to disappoint you both, but I'll keep my life. No matter how pathetic you think it is."

"I never said that! And I would never think that way about you. But that doesn't make what you did okay. You can't—"

"Don't assume he's stronger than me just because I'm in a wheelchair," he cut in. "That didn't stop me from kicking his ass before, and I can do it again if I have to."

"You beat him up?" I asked, bewildered. Was that how he'd ended up in a coma? I couldn't imagine him doing that when they'd just been in an accident. If he had, then he must be psychotic.

Devon's cold gaze chilled me. "Watch out, Hazel. I won't go easy on you if you team up with him."

I couldn't form words as he spun away and headed for the door. Hadn't he kissed me just a few hours ago? I hadn't hallucinated that, had I? Because he was acting like it had never happened and...threatening me? Yes, that had definitely been some kind of a threat.

"What is happening?" Abby demanded. "How did he know you were here, and who were you talking about?"

I found my voice, and it sounded stronger than I expected. "That's a good question! I thought that I was just imagining talking to him when I was...in a trance or whatever, but I must have really connected with him—and he somehow found me here through that."

She stared at me, wide-eyed. "You mean you talked to Devon using your psychic powers, like in The Shining?"

I winced, wishing that she hadn't used a horror movie to describe what had happened. "Yes, like that."

"That's amazing!" a girl at the table beside us exclaimed. She hadn't been there before my psychic session, so she must have arrived during or after it. "I thought Salem was going to be boring, because who cares what happened three hundred years ago? But I didn't know there were still real witches here. Were you born a witch or can anyone become one?"

She was obviously a tourist. I guessed her to be about fourteen, and there was a woman with her that I assumed was her mother. The lady was no help, since she was watching me with just as much fascination and curiosity as her daughter.

"You have to be born one," Abby said before I could tell them that I wasn't a witch. She stood up and pushed her chair in, prompting me to do the same.

We grabbed our drinks and started for the exit. Unfortunately, the girl jumped up and followed us. "Wait! Can you tell me if Noah likes me?"

Abby turned to her. "Who cares? He's not your destiny. You're going to do great things once you start paying attention in school. And you're going to meet the man of your dreams after you graduate from college."

The girl was hanging on her every word with a dreamy look in her eyes. "Wow. What's his name?"

"You'll know him when you meet him. But he likes smart girls, so study and do your best in school. You don't want to miss out on your destiny over something stupid."

"I will! I mean, I won't. I mean, I'll be ready for my destiny. Thank you so much!"

I gave Abby the side-eye when we got outside. "Can you tell me my fortune too?"

She shrugged. "Hey, I motivated her to do better in school. That's a much better goal than obsessing over some boy."

"It is," I agreed, thinking about how long I'd been obsessed with Devon. What had that gotten me besides heartache?

"Now tell me what happened," Abby demanded and sipped her drink.

"Wait until we get in the car."

I'd borrowed my mom's car when she got home from work, telling her that Abby needed cheering up after her close call with death. I hated using that as an excuse, but I wasn't about to reveal to my mother that Abby and I were going in search of a witch so I could get rid of a demon.

Except he wasn't.

"He did that to his twin?" Abby exclaimed in disbelief. "Aren't twins supposed to be even closer than regular brothers and sisters?"

"That's what I always heard too. But the cliché of the evil twin came from somewhere."

"Now you think that Devon is evil? Did you forget that he saved your life? And mine. Why would he do that if he was a bad person?"

I looked out the windshield at the fading light. Darkness was fast approaching, and we needed to get home soon. "I don't know. Maybe he's not all bad. I mean, he didn't kill his twin. He's obviously the same age as Devon."

"Hazel, this whole thing sounds made up. Getting the doctor to go along with it? And what about the people at the funeral home? Don't you think they would have noticed that they were missing a body? Did they just lie to Mr. Culver so they could sell him a coffin and make more money?"

My attention snapped back to her. "You're right. I didn't think about that." Confused, I added, "But what about Devon talking about him getting his inheritance? His brother would be the only one who could get that."

She thought about it for a moment and admitted that she had no explanation. "You've got me there. But I still don't believe that crazy story. Also, if his brother is alive, where's he been all this time?"

A shiver of dread ran down my spine. "He says Devon has him trapped, and he needs my help."

"How can you help him if you don't know where he is?"

I hesitated, unsure myself. "Maybe if I talk to him again, he'll be able to give me enough clues to figure it out. Then I can call the police to rescue him."

Abby's eyes narrowed as she thought. "Didn't Devon say that doing that makes him stronger?"

I remembered that too. "That doesn't make any sense. How could it make him stronger? He's making that up to keep me from finding out where he is."

"What if he's a demon? Doing this mind connecting thing with him could be dangerous. What if he possesses you?"

I gave her a deadpan look. "How can he get Devon's inheritance if he possesses me?"

"Oh, right. That doesn't make any sense," she admitted. "But I still don't like this, Hazel. You shouldn't be messing with this kind of stuff."

"You're the one who said I should use my psychic powers," I reminded her. "Ha! Can you believe I have psychic powers?"

She didn't share in my amazement over that. "I said to use them to find a witch. Did you even look for a witch?"

"I was going to, but I got sidetracked by Devon and his twin."

"Well, I think that you need to try again. You need help from someone who knows about this stuff."

My phone rang, and I glanced at the screen. "It'll have to wait until next time. My mom is calling me to come home."

Abby snatched my hand as I reached for my phone. My startled gaze flew to her intense one. "Promise me that you won't talk to him by yourself."

"Yeah, I promise," I said quickly, anxious to answer my mom's call.

It was a promise I broke, because I couldn't leave someone who needed my help waiting. If I was trapped somewhere, I'd want to be rescued as soon as possible. What kind of conditions was he in? Were they terrible? Did he have enough to eat and drink? He looked perfectly healthy in my dreams, but was that his real physical state?

Beyond helping him, I had to know the truth about Devon. Was the guy I'd been half in love with for years a monster who could do such a thing to his own brother? Could he truly be that evil?

My heart said no, but could I trust my heart? It wanted more kisses from him, even after he'd rejected me. It wanted us to be together and forget this whole thing about his twin. My heart was selfish and delusional and foolishly hopeful that we could still work things out. It had kept me pining after him even after I had found a wonderful boyfriend.

A boyfriend I hadn't deserved or appreciated. A boyfriend I had left to die when I went off with Devon as soon as he showed me the slightest bit of attention.

No, I couldn't rely on my heart to lead me in the right direction. I wasn't going to let another person suffer because my heart was urging me away from him. I knew why I was so reluctant to get in contact with him again. It was probably the same reason I had found him creepy in my dreams. A part of me must have known that he would destroy my delusions about Devon.

And Devon had warned me that he wouldn't go easy on me if I did this. I didn't know what that meant, but it made me even more anxious to get it done as soon as possible. He'd had his own brother declared dead, so what would he do to me? I had to stop him before he got the chance.

I said goodnight to my parents and pretended like I was going to sleep. I didn't change out of my clothes though, and I sat down on my floor instead of getting into bed. Taking a few slow, deep breaths helped to calm me a little. I tried to ignore the dread that was gathering in my empty stomach. Since I'd come home so late in the evening, I'd had to lie that I'd eaten dinner at Abby's house.

How much I wished that was true, and that we'd had a normal visit just talking about everything that was going on. It occurred to me that I hadn't even asked her about what had happened with Kyle. Had he told her that he liked her and asked her out? And what about the rest of our friends? I hadn't bothered to talk to Emily and see how she was coping after being so shaken up by Abby's close call with death.

Tomorrow, I promised myself. Tomorrow I would stop being so selfish and show my friends that I cared about them. I would be there for them—no matter what happened tonight.

But first, I had to get this done.

Without Abby here to hold my hands and anchor me, I felt very alone. This had seemed silly in the coffee shop, but it was kind of scary now. Of course, that was ridiculous. I was safe in my house, in my familiar room with the lights on. My parents were home and close by if I needed them. But I wouldn't. Because nothing could hurt me here. I was just scaring myself over nothing. I closed my eyes and breathed deeply.

Then I reached out for him with my mind.

CHAPTER 10

t was instantaneous, like he had been waiting for me. "I knew you would do it," he said, sounding gleeful.

Unease skittered down my spine, and I chided myself. Of course he would be happy to be rescued. "Do you have any idea where you are? Is it a house, or an apartment? Anything you can tell me will help the police find you."

"You can find me yourself," he declared. "All you have to do is open your mind to me."

"Uh, my mind is already open to you. That's why I can hear you—in my mind."

"No, more like at the edge of your mind. The best way I can describe it is that it's like you're talking to me through a screen door. I'm right outside, but you haven't let me in yet."

"But I don't know how to do that!" I exclaimed. "I didn't even know I could do this much until today."

He spoke in a disapproving tone. "Powers like yours, and you haven't used them? Well, they will no longer go to waste. Take down that barrier and let me in."

I concentrated extra hard. "Did it work?"

"Of course not," he snapped. "Do you feel anything different?"

"I'm sorry. I'm trying, but I don't know how to do it. Maybe you should try describing where you are."

"No!" he exclaimed angrily. "You're not going to quit when we're so close."

I wanted to snap back at him, but I reminded myself that he needed my help. That was why he was being so short-tempered with me. He was frustrated that this rescue attempt wasn't working.

Excitement suddenly replaced my annoyance. "Oh, I feel it! Like a fluttering at the edge of my mind. Is that you? How do I let you in?"

"No, that's that worthless fly buzzing around you and trying to get in our way. Whatever you do, don't let him in."

"Devon?" I said in alarm. "What are we going to do now? How does he always know when I'm talking to you?"

"He knows because he and I are connected, as much as we both hate it. But I'm going to sever that connection with your help. All you need to do is let me in. The only thing holding you back is your fear. Let go of it and free yourself to combine your power with mine. I'm not going to hurt you. Just the opposite in fact. You'll be stronger with me than you ever thought possible."

It was my panic over Devon's presence at the periphery of my mind that propelled me to drop the barrier between me and *him*. I still didn't know his name, because I had forgotten to ask him. That didn't stop him from gliding in with malevolent grace and glory. He was a dark prince of destruction, terrifying but regal and beautiful at the same time.

Too late, I realized that he was a demon after all.

"Not a demon. I'm your other half, whole, the way I was meant to be."

"So, you *are* Devon's twin." *Except you're the evil one*, I thought.

"Is it evil to want to live?" he demanded. "Even that pathetic shell wants that. Which was why he was so desperate to summon me into existence. Except he was too much of a coward to pay the price."

"Devon brought you back to life?" I asked in amazement.

He laughed, apparently finding that extremely funny. "Oh, my sweet, naïve girl; you are giving him too much credit. You think he was trying to raise his brother from the dead? That thought never entered his selfish head."

"Because it's impossible," Devon said. "Nobody can bring someone back from the dead."

"Ah, good, you've joined us. I'm glad you're here to defend yourself, so Hazel is left under no delusions about who you really are. The point is that you never even tried. You only thought of yourself."

I could see both of them now, because we were all in the void together. I wasn't sure how that was possible, since I thought we were talking through our minds. But they were speaking with their mouths now, and so was I. At the back of my mind, I wondered if we had been physically transported here.

"What is going on?" I demanded. "Devon, who is this guy?"

"Who is he? You didn't bother to find that out before you joined forces with him to kill me?"

"Kill you?" I exclaimed in bewilderment. "What are you talking about?"

"Oh, did I forget to mention that?" Devon's doppelganger asked.

I stared at him in horror, while he was clearly enjoying himself.

"You see," he continued, "it's physics. Two identical objects cannot occupy the same space at the same time."

I was completely confused now. "I have no idea what you're saying."

It was Devon who answered. "He's saying that he has to kill me to take over my life."

"It's actually my life, and I can live it better than you. Isn't that why you called me forth?"

"No, it's my life! I just wanted..."

"To be me?" his lookalike suggested.

"No," Devon refuted, but he looked defeated. "I wanted to be like I was before."

Sudden understanding had my heart breaking for him. He meant before the accident, before he was paralyzed. "You did a spell to heal yourself."

His gaze shifted away from me, hiding the vulnerability in his eyes that I'd never seen there before. I respected his privacy and turned my attention to the other guy. "What are you?"

That rankled his smooth demeanor. "I'm not a what," he snapped. "I'm a person—Devon Culver."

I huffed in annoyance. "Stop lying. *He's* Devon. If you're not his twin, then who are you?"

"I'm the real Devon, the one that I was supposed to be. Not that defective version."

"Stop calling him that! And stop lying! I know the real Devon, and you're not him."

"He is," Devon said. "He is me, or at least a part of me."

I looked at him and shook my head. "No, he's bad. I sensed it before, but I can really feel it now. He's got this dark energy that's nothing like yours."

"Because his energy is as weak as he is," fake Devon said.

"It was strong enough to kick your ass," Devon shot back.

"Stop bickering and explain this to me," I demanded.

Devon sighed. "I thought at first that the spell had worked. I felt this strange sensation everywhere—even my legs. I thought I was about to get up and walk, but something pulled out of my body instead. And then *he* was standing there, and I was still in my wheelchair."

"Now he's admitted it to you himself that I'm his true self. So, you won't have to mourn him."

He said it so matter-of-factly that it took a moment for me to grasp the chilling meaning of his words. He couldn't be serious!

But one glance at Devon's grim expression told me that he was. I slowly faced fake Devon, who had a content look on his face. It wasn't the expression I'd expected to see on someone who'd just threatened to murder a person.

"It's not murder if I kill myself. Actually, I'm just replacing the old me with a new, improved version."

"This is crazy. You don't need his life. Just live your life and let him live his," I pleaded.

"You still don't understand. We are not separate people who can live separate lives in this world. There is only one body I can inhabit, and I can't do that if it's already occupied."

I pointed my finger at him. "You *are* a demon! You're trying to possess him!"

He rolled his eyes. "Back to that again."

"And you read my mind," I exclaimed, having just realized it. "I was thinking about you not looking like a murderer, and you answered me like I said it out loud."

"Because you let me in, remember? You can read my mind too if you stop holding yourself back."

I recoiled from the very thought of it. Who knew what kind of evil thoughts were in his mind? And he was a guy. Didn't they supposedly think about sex all the time? I sure didn't want to know those thoughts. I might be scarred for life.

He laughed. "You're adorable. No wonder Devon is so enamored with you."

My gaze shot to Devon, hoping to see the truth of those words, but his pained expression seemed to confirm his rejection of me.

"Don't worry, I'll take good care of her," fake Devon said. "She'll have everything she wants. Diamonds and designer clothes, a luxury car and a driver to take her anywhere she needs to go, and absolutely the best of everything. I'm going to increase the family fortune and make us the wealthiest people in America. You could never accomplish that. She'll be far better off with me."

Devon pinned his dark, intense gaze on him. "You promise not to hurt her?"

Fake Devon appeared to be genuinely perplexed. "Why would I hurt her? We're a perfect match, as you well know. I'm truly impressed that you resisted her for as long as you did. She's like the constant pull of a magnet."

"You feel that too?" Devon asked in surprise.

"Of course. I am you in all the ways." He glanced down at his wheelchair. "Except one."

Devon nodded, his expression settling into a look of acceptance.

I was still processing their conversation when I felt the power being drawn out of me. It was invisible, but I knew exactly where it was going. It was traveling along the gateway I'd opened to fake Devon, making him stronger. His eyes were locked with Devon's, the two of them focused completely on each other.

Cold fear seized me as I realized what Devon was doing—staring death in the face. He was going to die, and he wasn't going to fight it. And it was all my fault. This time it was really my fault. I'd let this monster trick me and take my power, and he was going to use it to kill Devon and take over his life.

I had to stop this! Focusing with all my might, I tried to reverse the flow of power and draw it back into me. But it didn't work. Either I didn't know how to do it, or fake Devon was stronger than me.

Or it's too late, he told me in my mind. *Look away, Hazel*.

But I couldn't look away as I stared helplessly at Devon. Tears gathered in my eyes as I felt the power gathering in his nemesis as he prepared to strike him down.

He was going to die because of me. Because of *me*.

There was no time to think or debate what to do. I made a split-second decision and threw myself in front of Devon just as his enemy unleashed the full force of our combined power.

"Hazel, no!" I heard them shout in unison.

Then I heard a horrible scream, but I didn't know whose it was. There was a blinding flash of unbearable pain that was mercifully cut short, like a candle flame being blown out.

Then there was nothing.

―――

MIDNIGHT FLOWER

This is a vampire love story in a poem I wrote years ago. I thought someone might enjoy it, since it is also a paranormal romance.

Midnight Flower

She plunged into the woods just before twilight.
Tears of despair blurred her sight.
Unheeding of where she tread,
She was consumed by the images in her head.

All that remained to her was a drunken father.
Today they had laid to rest her beloved mother.
Isabella did not notice the dwindling light.
Further and further she walked into the night.

With no solace to be found,
She wandered far from familiar ground.
Peering through the trees at the night sky,
She continued to wonder why.

The moon slipped behind a misty veil.
The silence was broken by a voice distinctly male.

What seek you here at this late hour?
He spoke with authority and power.

Out of the shadows came a cloaked stranger.
She was too weary to fear any danger.
His eyes held an unnatural gleam.
She recalled tales of those who are not what they
seem.

These woods are not safe at night to roam.
I shall see you safely home.
Now he will take me to his lair.
She should be frightened, but she did not care.

This hour would be her last.
She spoke freely to him of her past.
When she shivered, he gave her his cloak.
He listened in silence to every word she spoke.

He led her back to the edge of the woods to her
surprise.
For a fleeting moment she thought she saw amuse-
ment in his eyes.
The night had softened now just before dawn.
When she turned to thank him, he was gone.

She returned home and quickly hid the cloak.
Her father would not see it when he awoke.
She thought of the stranger all that long day.
She would return the cloak as soon as she could slip
away.

Isabella went first to her mother's grave.
Her tender company she did crave.
To her spirit now she spoke,
Telling her about the stranger and the cloak.

She waited until the sun was setting low.
Into the woods she again did go.
When darkness fell the stranger soon was found.
He was suddenly there when she turned around.

> *I did not expect your return.*
> *Caution you did not learn.*
> *Isabella handed him the cloak.*
> *Her anger he did not provoke.*

I came to thank you and to return this.
She spoke as if nothing were amiss.
I wanted to see you again, truth be told.
Her curiosity about him had made her bold.

For both of us this decision is unwise.
Yet I cannot turn away from your innocent eyes.
You charm me with your lack of guile.
You should know my name is Stefan if we are to
*   visit awhile.*

Being with him lessened her pain.
In small increments her loneliness did wane.
She came to see him for a few hours every night.
Soon in his presence her heart took delight.

A man in her village sought her as his prey.
She did not see him follow her that day.
The sun was sinking as he fell upon her.
Isabella struggled against the filthy cur.

> *He tore at her clothes*
> *As she bloodied his nose.*
> *A lively one, he sneered.*
> *All was lost she feared.*

*Stefan advanced on him with fury, his face feral
    and wild.
He picked him up as if he weighed no more than a
    child.
Sharp fangs sank deep as he drank his fill.
Her attacker now lay pale and still.*

*Isabella began to thank him, but he stopped her
    dead.
He spoke with lips that were stained blood red.
You were attacked because of me.
You are in a place you should not be.*

*Now you know that I am a monster most vile,
A danger to all who linger here awhile.
Isabella pulled him into a fierce embrace.
A look of adoration was on her face.*

*You have been no danger to me.
Only one monster here did I see.
You have slain him dead.
Your company I do not dread.*

*Stefan sent her home to rest.
He would see her tomorrow at her request.
The next day her father told her she was to wed.
At nightfall back to Stefan she fled.*

*Stefan said it was probably for the best.
Isabella declared it was a life she would detest.
Emboldened by a love so rare,
She did that which she did not dare.*

*Stefan was the one who ended the kiss.
She said to him, I want only this.
You know not what you ask, Stefan said.*

Sunrise brings me the slumber of the dead.

I know I want to be with you for eternity.
Nothing else matters to me.
What does a girl of fifteen know of eternity?
Begone! Leave me be.

I will not marry him. I would rather be dead.
All that night bitter tears she shed.
The next night she again went Stefan to find.
She had to make him change his mind.

I cannot abide your sorrow.
You are leaving here tomorrow.
Arrangements for you I have made.
The ticket for your journey has been paid.

I will stay with you until just before dawn.
By seven your train will be gone.
Do not think that you will find me here.
I lingered only because you were near.

This is not where I dwell.
I have remained too long under your spell.
You shall have a new home.
No longer these woods will you roam.

After much arguing, Isabella gave up the fight.
This was not how she wanted to spend their last
*   night.*
Now Stefan told her the secrets of his past.
Their time together was over too fast.

He branded her lips with a kiss that was less than
*   chaste.*
Goodbye my love, he said and left in great haste.

Her chaperone she met when she boarded the train.
She would not be allowed to be alone with her pain.

A motherly companion she had until her long
    journey was done.
Then she was deposited into the care of a greatly
    older one.
Servants brought in luggage she never knew
    she had.
Even such fine clothes could not keep her from
    being sad.

A companion she was to a spry old lady.
Every day they talked while sharing tea.
Lessons she had in reading, writing, and dancing,
    too.
She learned all the things that a fine lady knew.

Your benefactor desires that you be presented at a
    ball.
My benefactor! Has he come to call?
No, my dear, he has written to me.
A letter. May I see?

    I'm afraid not. He values his privacy.
    Come, my dear. Do not frown.
    You are to have an exquisite new gown.
    The ball would be her entrance to society.
    Surely Stefan would be there to see.

    Isabella became a sensation that night.
    Her hair was the color of pale moonlight.
    Many suitors she did attract,
    Save for the one her heart lacked.

Stefan was not coming for her. This she had to
     accept.
After the ball she threw herself on her bed and wept.
In the months after that by many proposals she was
     not persuaded.
Her suitors gave up, but one fine young man was
     not dissuaded.

Of her new husband her heart soon grew fond,
Although she never forgot her secret bond.
Often in her dreams Stefan did appear.
Other times she gazed out into the night and imag-
     ined he was near.

Over the years four babies filled her arms.
She was content with her life's many charms.
When her youngest daughter turned fifteen,
She awoke in the night and felt a presence unseen.

Isabella slipped out of bed and found Stefan
     outside.
Her shock she could not even try to hide.
She was beginning to go gray.
He had aged not a single day.

No, do not thank me.
Stefan smiled bitterly.
I am here selfishly,
Although I swore to let you be.

What I do now I cannot defend.
It tortures me to think that your life will end.
I bring you a vial of my cursed blood.
It can turn back the tide of death's flood.

Once the change has begun,

It can never be undone.
Think very carefully.
The decision stands for eternity.

Isabella kept the vial hidden away.
This she would decide on a distant day.
Time brought her the joy of watching her grand-
    children play.
Life drifted on in this pleasant way.

Now even her grandchildren were grown.
Since John died, five years she had been alone.
A lifetime they had shared.
He had been a sweet man who truly cared.

She was up in age,
Left to contemplate this final stage.
Staring at the vial had become her nightly game.
After all these years, the scarlet liquid looked
    exactly the same.

Isabella thought about what countless lifetimes with
    Stefan would mean.
Although her body was deteriorating, her mind was
    still keen.
A monster Stefan had claimed to be.
He fed only on evildoers. She had long since had
    this epiphany.

Isabella opened the vial and drank.
Into a deep slumber she quickly sank.
When she opened her eyes, she was wide awake.
She stood before the mirror a look to take.

She stared in shock, stiff as a board.
Her youth had been completely restored.

———

Thank you for reading! Hazel and Devon's story continues in Haunted World, available now. If you would like to read Devon's side of the story, Haunted Magic is available now.

www.ingramcontent.com/pod-product-compliance
Lightning Source LLC
Chambersburg PA
CBHW031546310726
48971CB00008B/2640